**Bolton
Council**

Please return/renew this item
by the last date shown.
Books may also be renewed by
phone or the Internet.

BX

**Tel: 01204 332384
www.bolton.gov.uk/libraries**

PHANTOM

Newcastle based lawyer Eric Ward is surprised when an important local shipping firm, Goldwaters, pay him a large retainer to do some work for them. A Goldwaters ship, the *Sierra Nova*, has been 'arrested' and is unable to leave the port. The reason given is that one of the crew, Edwards, has been caught smuggling drugs – but now he's been removed from the ship, why can't the voyage go ahead? Things get even more complicated when Edwards is killed on his way into the courtroom. Ward soon finds himself immersed in the dangerous world of international conspiracy and modern day piracy.

PHANTOM

PHANTOM

by

Roy Lewis

Magna Large Print Books
Long Preston, North Yorkshire,
BD23 4ND, England.

British Library Cataloguing in Publication Data.

A catalogue record of this book is
available from the British Library

ISBN   978-0-7505-4486-3

First published in Great Britain in 2002 by Allison & Busby Limited

Cover illustration © Silvrshootr by arrangement with iStock

The right of Roy Lewis to be identified as author of this work has been
asserted by him in accordance with the Copyright, Designs and
Patents Act, 1988

Published in Large Print 2018 by arrangement with Roy Lewis

Magna Large Print is an imprint of Library Magna Books Ltd.

Printed and bound in Great Britain by
T.J. (International) Ltd., Cornwall, PL28 8RW

Prologue

A light breeze whispered off the South China Sea, bringing a cool relief in the sultry tropical darkness to the man who lounged against the rail on the deck of the cargo ship *Pulau Tengah*. The heat of the day had been intense, as always; thunderclouds had gathered above Batam at four that afternoon, but although the skies had blackened threateningly and flickering stabs of distant lightning had illuminated the gloom above the turgid sea, the anticipated storm had not broken and the weather had been humid, the air close and stifling, men dripping with sweat as they prepared the cargo ship for the voyage.

They had sailed with the tide, cargo-less, the crew of seven men anticipating a short, trouble-free voyage into Malaysian jurisdiction. Once they left Indonesian waters a feeling of relief crept over them and their mood lightened now the edge of danger had dissipated. They passed the glittering lights of Singapore and turned north; off Johor they dropped anchor; and now it was only a matter of waiting for a few hours until the agent came on board later that night, to bring the appropriate documentation and advise the skipper on the arrangements for delivery of the *Pulau Tengah* to its new, Malaysian owner. There was now time to relax, enjoy the respite, contemplate what they might do with the money that was coming to them, open the brandy and the beer and the whisky.

Charlie Minh was shirtless as he leaned on the rail, his dark, lean-muscled back gleaming with the sheen of sweat as he drew on the reefer and contemplated the glittering stars in the black sky high above the deck. There had been a current of edginess during this last voyage: the skipper had been nervy as though expecting trouble, but there had been none, they had delivered the cargo safely at Batam with no interference from Indonesian navy launches, and now they had left the dangerous waters and could relax. No cargo, no worries, a job well completed. Charlie's task was to keep watch, but they were safe in Malaysian waters, protected by bribes already paid; he drew on his reefer, hearing the noise of the carousing below deck and regretting that it had fallen to him to maintain the watch. He could have done with a few cold beers.

He left the rail, wiping his face with a greasy bandana, sat down, leaned back against a hatch cover. He dreamed for a little while of the days of his youth in the *kampong* in mountainous Sabah, below the typhoon belt, the Land Below the Wind, but then his thoughts soon drifted to the woman he and the rest of the crew had all enjoyed only a few days earlier. It had been a bonus: the family had been drifting, a small boatload of economic migrants heading blindly out to sea, expecting to be picked up by the people they had paid handsomely to transfer them aboard a cargo ship, so they could be taken on the long journey to Australia. They had been hoping to avoid the

10

Australian navy and land on the wild northern shore for a better life. Charlie Minh bared stained teeth in a vicious grin: the worries of the would-be emigrants were over now. The *Pulau Tengah* had plucked them out of the wind-whipped sea in which they were drifting, sinking, desperate. What few valuables they possessed had been torn from them, the two men, the old woman and the child had been quickly despatched, thrown overboard, while the young woman had been detained on board the *Pulau Tengah,* for a few, pleasurable hours. His body stirred at the memory: she had been young, inexperienced before they had taken turns with her. Charlie wished now that the skipper had not been so strict, insisting that when they were all sated she also should be consigned to the waters, her throat cut, like the others. Charlie thought they could have kept her with them for a few days more, maybe hidden her below decks while they unloaded at Batam, so she would be available to them again now that the business was done, and the tension eased. He glared at the glowing end of his reefer: there were times when he hated the skipper with a fierce resentment, and this was one of them.

He put his head back against the hatch, flicked the stub of the reefer over the side, watching the glowing end as it arced towards the dark water and then he sighed, closed his eyes. He thought still about the woman, the bitten breasts under his mouth, the gleaming sheen of her exhausted, spiritless body as she had lain under him, submissive, defeated, shuddering as he laboured to sexual climax...

11

He awoke with a start. For a moment his wits were skittering in the darkness, his heart hammering in thoughtless panic. He blinked, not understanding what had woken him; next moment he felt something slide down his cheek, press against his jaw. There was a terrifying coldness to the steel barrel of the pistol pressed against his mouth. He sat motionless, stiff with terror, his eyes wide and glaring at the dark-clothed, whispering figure who stood over him.

'Not a sound, my friend, or you join your ancestors with no roof to your dirty mouth.'

Charlie Minh's eyes rolled as he saw the dark figures, rubber-soled, drop silently to the deck, climbing from the launch that had drawn alongside, undetected in the sultry darkness as he had slept and dreamed. A few muttered orders, and the well-drilled men were spreading out, heading for the companionway that led to the lower deck, and to the sounds of the drunken carousal below. There was nothing Charlie could do to warn the crew; nothing he *wanted* to do, with the pistol bruising his gums, pressing hard against his stained teeth.

It was all over very quickly. There was a sudden burst of warning gunfire, the crashing of doors, the stampeding of feet. Charlie heard the sound of smashing glass as bottles were thrown, a confused, drunken shouting arose, but Charlie knew that no one below would have been prepared for action, not here, not off Johor, in the Malacca Straits, where the protection money had long since been paid.

The pistol muzzle clattered painfully against

Charlie's teeth. 'Get below. Join the others.'

Charlie obeyed without a word, scrambling to his feet wildly, heading for the companionway. He glanced over the side: the launch was already moving away into the darkness, its wake silvering in the intermittent moonlight. He half-stumbled into the mess room where the other six were being held, huddled sullenly on their haunches, hands clasped above their heads. He stared at the men standing there and he started with surprise: he recognised one of the men who had boarded the *Pulau Tengah,* and who was standing beside a man who held a machine pistol on the crew. Their eyes met and the man smiled thinly, teeth gleaming above his wispy beard. 'Hello, Charlie, still keeping in with bad company, hey?'

Cheung Kiat, ex-captain of the *Pulau Tengah.*

Charlie glared around him. He was beginning to understand, as he heard the armed cadre moving about purposefully, searching the ship. There was a slight shading of relief in his veins: he had been expecting something worse, a quick knife across his throat, a painful gutting before he was thrown overboard. But these men were not what he had expected. They were heavily armed navy personnel. This was not a hijacking. This was a planned raid by the Malaysian navy.

The burly, heavy-faced man with the black moustache who stepped into the silent mess room bore an unmistakeable air of authority. He looked around the huddled group then nodded towards Charlie. 'This man was on watch?'

Cheung Kiat nodded, licking his lips above a trembling beard. 'His name's Charlie Minh.'

'Get the rest of them in irons. He goes back on deck.'

'You find what was expected, sir?' Cheung Kiat asked eagerly.

The burly naval officer stared at him sourly. 'Your information was correct, just as well for you. We've found handcuffs, balaclavas, bayonets, *parangs*, AK 47s. False documents, Honduran flag, paint, date stamps...' His cold, hooded eyes flickered towards Charlie Minh. 'And a speedboat with a two hundred horsepower engine. All the stock in trade we'd expect.'

Cheung Kiat licked his lips in nervous relief. 'And now we wait?'

'We wait.' The naval officer flicked a hostile glance at Charlie Minh. 'We wait like the cat, until the mouse comes on board. And you,' he nodded at Charlie, 'will get above again – and do just what the mouse expects.'

On deck, Charlie shivered in spite of the sultriness of the night air. Behind him, in the darkness there were two men with machine pistols. The sea held no prospect of escape: they were too far from shore. His teeth chattered as he thought of what lay in store for him. There might be a chance to live, if he did as Cheung Kiat had done, and became a turncoat. Or maybe Cheung Kiat had always worked, even when he was captain of the *Pulau Tengah,* as a police informer. But what did Charlie Minh have to offer them that they did not already have? He was just a crew member: he had no special information, and what he could tell them would do him no credit. He thought of the woman, throat cut, body abused, dropping silently

14

over the side and he began to shake. Someone would inevitably talk about that: it would come out. Afterwards, it would be the hell hole of prison for a while ... and then execution.

He slumped against the rail, his head dropping. The moon drifted out from behind dark clouds, and he caught the brief gleam of steel in the hands of one of the navy guards. There was nothing he could do, but wait, play his part. He was helpless.

They all stood there in the darkness of the lifting deck for two hours, silent, grim. The ship rode softly at anchor, sliding gently in the swell. Charlie Minh's pulse slowed: he was now resigned. The excitement and the pleasure, the killing, whoring, violence and drunkeness were now over for him. He was still scared, but he had to think of what was the best way forward for himself. And he owed nothing to the man who would be coming aboard. Nor did he have regrets. But he wished they had kept that woman just a little longer...

The first faint purring sound off to starboard was like a light soughing of the wind among distant palm trees. The sound changed into a low, throaty, controlled throbbing. Charlie stood at the rail, swallowing dryly, as an order was growled at him. He was to do what was expected. Charlie picked up the torch and as he saw the dimmed lights pause, the launch heave to some hundred metres distant, he flicked on the torch briefly, three short flashes, and a longer one.

After a tense moment, the launch came forward again, its engines subdued, careful, ready to burst into full throttle at the first hint of trouble. Charlie waved the torch in long, slow arcs. He owed nothing to this man; there was no reason why he should not suffer the same fate that awaited Charlie Minh.

Within minutes the dark launch was bumping softly against the hull of the *Pulau Tengah*. Charlie Minh extended a hand to the swarthy man with the suspicious eyes; moments later the Chinese man came on board. There was a short, expectant pause, then a scraping clanging sound from their left. With a muffled oath the swarthy Indonesian dragged out a handgun as the navy personnel came swarming forward but it was too late: he was quickly overpowered and he glared at Charlie, spitting out oaths. The Chinese man, small, slight, light cotton-suited, bald head gleaming under the fitful moon, raised his startled hands above his waist, saying nothing. He was bundled roughly down the companionway, Charlie thrust down after him along with the swarthy gunman.

The Malaysian naval officer was waiting in the main cabin. There was another man with him now, a westerner Charlie had not seen earlier. He was tall, well-muscled, fit, perhaps in his late thirties, clad in jeans and dark sweater. His skin was tanned by exposure to the sea breezes of the Pacific Rim; his thinning fair hair was cut *en brosse;* he had clear, piercing blue eyes and the hard, relentless mouth of a man for whom tenacity of purpose was a way of life. The Chinese man let out a slow breath of recognition. 'Mr Michaels.'

'Mr Lee,' the fair-haired man acknowledged.

'Your presence here...?'

'I work for the International Maritime Bureau,' Michaels explained coldly.

'The IMB...' Mr Lee sighed, shook his head in slow consternation. 'Hah, I should have realised...' The Chinese man's words were marked by his quiet, regretful tone.

There was a short silence. Charlie Minh, forgotten, stood against the bulkhead as the two protagonists faced each other. He recognised the accent of the westerner: Charlie Minh had had more than a few wild drunken evenings with brothel-bound Australians in various landfalls along the Pacific Rim. 'So,' the man called Michaels was saying with a slight, cynical smile on his lips, 'perhaps there is an explanation for the arrival on board the *Pulau Tengah* of a Singapore shipping agent, in the dead of night–'

'The life of a shipping agent is a busy one,' Mr Lee commented, lifting a negligent, cotton-suited shoulder, 'and must fall in with the requirements of his clients.'

'Even when the ship he boards holds all the evidence and stock in trade of a piratical operation?'

The silence grew around them. Mr Lee smiled vaguely, took a deep breath, hooded his eyes thoughtfully, and then coughed, a rasping, throaty sound. 'Forgive me, the night airs... I was not, of course, aware that this ship might be carrying such ... evidence. My instructions are merely to arrange the documentation to deliver the *Pulau Tengah* to new owners based in–'

'We know where they're based,' Michaels interrupted in rough impatience. 'The fact is, now you're here, we're going to be able to have a number of deep conversations, and my expectation is that once we get you ashore you will be

17

able to furnish us with a lot of names in this organisation–'

Mr Lee coughed again. He waved a slim hand, deprecatingly. 'Please, your indulgence, this throat of mine...' He slipped his hand into his jacket pocket, and as the Malaysian naval officer stepped forward threateningly, he withdrew a small flat box of pastilles. 'Please, merely a patent remedy...'

'Not for all ills, I'm sure,' Michaels growled, shaking his head as Mr Lee opened the box, politely offered it to Michaels and then extracted a pastille and slipped it into his own mouth.

'For all ills of *this* world, I assure you,' Mr Lee commented blandly.

Michaels stared at him blankly for a moment, and then Charlie Minh saw alarm flare into the Australian's eyes. The man started forward, reaching out for Lee's throat but the eyes of Mr Lee were already glazed with determination as he clamped his jaws, biting into what he held in his mouth.

'Stop him!' Michaels snarled, clamping his hands on the Singaporean's jaws, forcing his mouth open but Charlie Minh knew the action was already too late. Within moments, Mr Lee was slumping forward. Michaels was holding him upright, they were trying to push back his head, force open his mouth. Charlie Minh, his bare shoulders against the sweating steel of the bulkhead, shivered at the intensity of the Singaporean's determination to meet his ancestors.

They laid the man down, finally. His body jerked spasmodically for a little while, then was still. There was the slight odour of bitter almonds in the cabin. The swarthy Indonesian bodyguard giggled in tension, not understanding.

Charlie Mirth, disregarded, stood frozen in terror against the bulkhead. The Singaporean must have greatly feared the people he worked for, to take cyanide rather than face the hostile questions of the International Maritime Bureau.

'Bloody hell,' the Australian called Michaels swore in furious frustration.

'*Inshallah*,' the Malaysian naval officer intoned philosophically, straightening up from the corpse of the Singaporean shipping agent. 'It is the will of Allah.'

Chapter One

When the court rose early Eric Ward made his way out to the Quayside and Wesley Square. The early frost had now dissipated in the weak morning sun, the rime that had glistened on the elegant sweeping arc of the Millennium Bridge had gone, and the rippling, wind-teased Tyne flowed dark blue under a spring sky. Gulls whirled, clamouring harshly above his head, as they competed for the dry crusts that were being thrown from the bridge by a party of schoolchildren and Eric sauntered along the quay for a few minutes, enjoying the crispness of the air, the salty tang of the light breeze soughing between the river banks, and the excited chattering of the school party crossing to the Gateshead landing.

He checked his watch. There were still ten minutes to go before he was due to meet Paul Sutherland at Goldwater & Sons, and it was only a short walk to their refurbished offices in the old Victorian warehouse near The Side. He had been surprised at the Goldwater call – he had had no previous dealings with the firm. He had checked them out, of course: their business was concentrated mainly on charters, it seemed, insurance and shipping contracts along the Tyne and into Norway. An old, well-established firm, but one with a relatively low profile, and he was a little surprised that they would be contacting him. Companies like Goldwaters tended to use their own, in-house lawyers, or larger legal firms in Newcastle and London for their business; Eric Ward's was a one man operation, with a client list somewhat on the seamy side, limited in scope, light on experience of major shipping activity and rarely used by the big operators on Tyneside.

'Maybe,' his loyal but occasionally tight-lipped secretary had suggested to him, 'this will give you an opportunity to get a somewhat better practice.' Susie Cartwright was forthright, outspoken, tall, forty and widowed and had never really approved of his willingness to deal with the low life along the river. She thought he – and she – deserved better things, and that Eric should have taken more advantage of the connections his wife had brought him. But at least Susie had maintained a sympathetic silence on the slow crumbling of his marriage. She had wanted to ask, he knew, but he was grateful that she had not done so.

The sudden thought of Anne, and their impending divorce removed some of the pleasure he was taking out of his surroundings. They were due to meet later in the week, with her solicitor John Elkins getting them together to discuss the financial arrangements consequent upon the divorce. Eric had thought the meeting unnecessary and had said so, but Anne had insisted that Elkins arrange it at his offices. Eric was dreading the occasion: he wanted no quarrelling over the detritus of the relationship; he and Anne had had a good marriage while it had lasted and he did not want memories bruised or distorted by squabbles over finance. He wanted nothing from the considerable estates she held, and though he had loved Sedleigh Hall, he knew it was time to move on. The tensions had become too great; he had always valued his independence, refused to be contaminated by the county circles she necessarily moved in, and if his secretary thought he was crazy refusing some of the opportunities that had come his way, that was her problem.

He leaned against the railing at the river's edge, and stared across to the looming Baltic warehouse, now being converted into a huge arts centre, amid the regeneration of the Gateshead bank. Still preoccupied with thoughts of Anne, he wondered whether Jason Sullivan QC would now be moving in with her at Sedleigh Hall. Somehow, he doubted it – he guessed she would take more time to determine the boundaries of that relationship. Eric still felt that Sullivan had been largely responsible for the break up of the marriage, but he was also aware of the corrosive part played by his own infidelity, and his own stubborn inability

21

to compromise, talk things through, open his heart to express his true feelings.

He shook his head, glanced at his watch. Time to move on. Time to set the past behind him, as far as he could. Time to go find out just what Goldwater & Sons had in store for him.

The echoing, marble-columned, cream-tiled entrance hallway was guarded by a uniformed receptionist who solemnly enquired of Eric which floor he required, and which company he wanted. Carefully, he entered Eric's name in a book, gave him a lapel badge and pointed him in the right direction. The lift was somewhat ancient, Victorian in construction, and creaky, but when Eric emerged on the third floor he was impressed by the standard of the refurbishment that had been undertaken by Goldwater & Sons. The former warehouse building had been gutted, he knew, to make way for new commercial enterprises that had been flooding into Newcastle with the regeneration of the Quayside, and the European money that had been pumped into the area, but it seemed that the companies that had come in, if the offices he was entering were anything to go by, were sparing no expense. The accommodation enjoyed by Goldwaters presented a marked contrast with his own premises: these were spacious, light, taking full advantage of the tail airy windows that gave a long view over older buildings clustered on the bank towards the sweeping bend of the Tyne. It was a far cry in elegance, if not distance, from his own office on the Quayside.

Nor did the reception staff bear much resemblance to his own Susie Cartwright. The young, blonde, tight-skirted woman who greeted him inside the high glass doors had a pleasant smile and manner, no hint of a Geordie accent, and touched his arm lightly as she ushered him immediately into a small boardroom where she offered him coffee. When he accepted, thanking her, she informed him it was *her* pleasure. The coffee was quickly made available, in light bone china.

From the window, Eric could see the midday traffic thundering over the Tyne Bridge, and the river as it glittered upstream under the Swing Bridge and beyond. The room itself was lined with books, unusually for a boardroom; he took a look along the shelves and discovered they were mainly old minute books and operational texts on marine insurance. He ran his hand along the top of the table, enjoying the high polished finish of the old mahogany, and noted that the chairs were of black, elegant, real leather. He heard the door open behind him and he put down his coffee cup, turned.

'Mr Ward? Sorry to keep you waiting. I'm Paul Sutherland.'

They shook hands. Sutherland was as tall as Eric but broader, younger, and probably fitter, his muscled chest filling the dark grey suit impressively. He had a lean face, finely chiselled features and hawkish, wary eyes: they held Eric's for several moments, summing up, but there was no warmth in the glance, and his handshake, though firm, was brief, almost perfunctory. He moved lightly for a big man, and Eric guessed that regular visits to a squash court or a workout facility would be part of his schedule. His hair was dark, neatly parted with a precision that he would no doubt apply to his business life. His voice was deep, his accent cut-glass public school, with no hint of a northern influence.

'Please, sit down, Mr Ward. You already have coffee, I see.'

'I've been well looked after, yes.'

'Good,' Sutherland replied indifferently, and took a seat at the head of the boardroom table, swivelling the chair, and placing his hands on the table in front of him. 'Your first visit here?'

'It is.'

'And we've not met before.' Sutherland nodded, crinkling his eyes thoughtfully. 'You've had no business contacts with Goldwaters previously.'

Eric shook his head. The room was silent, except for the low rumble of activity far below them in the Newcastle streets. Sutherland was frowning slightly, almost preoccupied; it was as though he was reluctant to develop the conversation, was biding his time, waiting for something, weighing up the consequences of what he was about to say. There was an edge of uncertainty in his manner that puzzled Eric, but he said nothing, waiting.

'Eric Ward,' Sutherland said abruptly. 'You have a law practice close by, here on the Quayside.'

'That's right.'

'And you were a policeman, before you took to the law.'

'That's correct.'

'You left the police because of ... physical problems.'

Eric involuntarily recalled the first cat-claw scratchings at the back of his eyes, years ago, when he went to see George Knox for a checkup. He had been told his condition meant his days in the force were numbered. It had led him to a new career as a solicitor, and indirectly a good marriage. He wondered why Sutherland thought it necessary to talk about his past. He nodded slightly, but made no reply. But he was keenly aware that Sutherland had done his homework, and that in itself was interesting.

Sutherland was staring at him with a certain accusatory belligerence. 'Your practice is mainly criminal.'

'Mainly, not entirely. I take what comes,' Eric replied easily. He shifted in his seat, crossed his legs casually. He was disinclined to try to impress Paul Sutherland. Though a little intrigued, he did not care for the man, there was something about him that grated on Eric, even after such brief acquaintance. As he stared at Sutherland, he even had the feeling he was somewhat disinclined to work for Goldwaters, if it meant developing a close relationship with the hard-eyed man who faced him.

Perhaps something of his feelings were communicated to Sutherland, who rubbed a nervous hand against his mouth. 'You'll gather I've been asking around.'

'That's clear to me. And I wonder why.'

'It's as well to know who one is dealing with. You're a one man practice, but I'm informed you're well-experienced, and your commitment to a client is regarded as ... sound. I've also been told that your ... discretion is assured.'

'That's the case with most lawyers,' Eric replied

25

lightly. 'It's part of the deal.'

'Legal privilege is really client privilege,' Sutherland nodded. Absently, he drummed his fingers on the table for a little while. Then, in an abrupt tone, he said, 'We have a problem here at Goldwaters.'

'Which your own lawyers can't handle?' Eric ventured.

Suspicion glittered in Sutherland's eyes. He hesitated, then shrugged. 'Our business is shipping. We have contracts throughout the world, though mainly in the Baltic countries. We're long-established, and the board ... well, they have a sense of history, they can be fuddy-duddy if you like, and they don't like some aspects of the new business world they've been forced to enter. The fact is, chartering has changed, Mr Ward, it's much more competitive, less gentlemanly, and more international in its ramifications. I was brought in a few years ago to deal with new, rising trends; the other executives on the board have tended to concentrate on the insurance side, where there's still good money to be earned. And that's where our lawyers have concentrated, too. And this business ... well. I consider it's not quite their line.'

'Whereas you consider it might be *my* kind of line,' Eric suggested.

'You could say that.' Sutherland clucked his tongue slightly. 'Horses for courses, as they say. You heard of the *Sierra Nova?*'

'I can't say that I have.'

'She's a three hundred tonne cargo ship, the subject of one of our charters, and she's been tied up at North Shields for the last six weeks.'

'Tied up?'

Sutherland struggled with the words. 'She's been arrested.'

There was a short silence.

Sutherland rose abruptly, turned to the long window and stared down at the river below. He locked his hands behind his back. 'Arrested. You know what that means, Ward? It means we can't move her, can't fulfil our commitments to the charterers, can't confirm onward charters, and that means a hell of a lot of money goes down the drain. All right, we've been on the fringe of such problems more than once – there are plenty of angry clients who will hold up a ship by claiming that the terms of the contract haven't been properly fulfilled, or insurance cover hasn't been adequate, or the dates on time charters have gone awry.' He turned back from the window, angrily. 'Our own lawyers are used to dealing with issues such as underwriting claims, bills of lading disputes, admiralty jurisdiction, short landings or implied terms, all that sort of thing. But the arrest of the *Sierra Nova,* it's different: it's something we haven't come across before, and frankly, we feel we need a new pair of eyes to look at the issues.'

'What are the issues?' Eric asked quietly.

Sutherland grunted in exasperation. 'That's the problem. We seem to be punching a bagful of feathers, trying to find out. We're being given the runaround by the local police, that's the beginning and end of it, in my view. The *Sierra Nova* was chartered through our agency in Bergen; she sailed to Rotterdam and then crossed the North Sea and berthed at Teesside. Then she came to the Tyne. But the moment she arrived at North

Shields all hell broke loose. She was placed under arrest, and that means she can't leave the dock, we can't fulfil the charter, and we have ongoing problems with new charters that could bring in astronomical losses. Not to mention the damage it does to the reputation of our firm.'

'What reason has been given for the ship arrest?' Eric asked, puzzled.

There was a short silence. Sutherland came back to the table, slouched into his seat, drummed his fingers on the table. He shook his head. 'Normally, these things are pretty straightforward. A civil matter. A misunderstanding. A lawsuit over a contract of affreightment, perhaps. Sometimes, it gets to the Admiralty court. We've no problem with all that: hell, we're insured against such contingencies. But this is different. I think the bloody ship has been arrested for the activities of one man!'

Eric raised his eyebrows. 'A crew member?'

Sutherland nodded bitterly. 'A man called Edwards. He's been arrested.'

'And so has the ship?'

Sutherland's glance held Eric's but there was nothing to be read in his eyes. 'Edwards was picked up for possession. Suspected of smuggling drugs.'

Eric leaned back in his chair, surprised. He was silent for a little while, thinking. He wondered just how much information Sutherland would, in the end, give him. He nodded slowly. 'So this crew member, Edwards, has been arrested, and charges brought. But what reason has been given for the ship arrest?'

Sutherland's mouth twisted. 'That's the problem. We're being given the runaround, Ward. Enquiries are proceeding, they say. Edwards is being questioned. Oh, they've come up with an immediate reason to hold the *Sierra Nova* – they say some of the documentation is not in order, that a bill of lading has been fraudulently misdated, that a creditor of the last charterer is seeking an *in rem* judgement, but that's all just bullshit! There's something going on that I – we – don't know about. I mean, this sailor Edwards, he didn't even join the crew until Amsterdam! I just feel this is some kind of setup. And that's where you come in.'

'What do you want from me?'

'I want to engage you to find out what the hell is going on, and to find out what we need to do to get the *Sierra Nova* clear to proceed as soon as possible.'

'Why do you think I can do it any better than your own lawyers?' Eric queried.

Sutherland stared at the table thoughtfully. 'I've already told you: our people are experts in charters and insurance ... but we've never hit this kind of problem before. That's one reason. There's another. You're local; you're small time. And you know the riverside. You've got contacts; I'm told that your years in the police have given you ... experiences other solicitors on Tyneside don't have. You have access to ... to the gossip that can swirl around the back streets. And you know how the police get on with their business.'

Eric waited. When the silence grew around them, he said, 'I wonder whether there isn't another reason for employing me.'

'Such as?'

'You tell me, Mr Sutherland.'

Paul Sutherland didn't like it; he glowered, clenched his fist in an involuntary spasm of irritation, but after a few moments he gave way. 'All right,' he snapped. 'The reasons I've given are sound, and they apply. This business is out of our lawyer's league, in my view. But there is another reason, I'll admit. And it's the reason why I want fast results.'

Eric waited.

Chewing at his lip, Sutherland went on. 'End of the month we have our usual board meeting, and it's followed by a meeting of the major shareholders. I have to give a report. I'll have to tell them what's happened to the *Sierra Nova*.'

'They don't already know?' Eric asked in surprise.

Sutherland made an angry, dismissive gesture with his left hand. 'They don't bother too much with the operational side. They're interested only in bottom line figures. They will have heard about the problem, of course, the reason given for the arrest. They think it's all financial. I'd like to keep them thinking that way. I don't want them getting all excited about the possibility of Goldwaters being involved in some kind of criminal activity.' A certain nervousness had crept into Sutherland's tone, undermining the early belligerent confidence.

'They don't know about this man Edwards.'

Sutherland shook his head. 'They don't need to. This is all a mistake. There's no reason why the *Sierra Nova* should be arrested just because a stash of cocaine was found in some bloody crewman's duffel bag, but that's what happened. And I want to know why. *Why* is this happening to me?'

So there was a personal element to it. A new contract coming up maybe, or a bonus in danger of being withdrawn. 'You want a resolution of the ... problem, before the end of the month,' Eric said slowly.

'I don't want the matter aired at the share-holders meeting,' Sutherland agreed in a flat tone. 'And I want some answers.'

'I still don't see how precisely I'll be able to help. A bigger law firm, better connected, could put on pressure in all the right places...'

'No. They'd be the *wrong* places,' Sutherland insisted in exasperation. 'We can access all the big noises on Tyneside, call in debts, make use of our contacts but they won't be able to help. And things ... would get out. You know how things are. If there's a sniff of anything ... awkward, people jump ship in droves.'

'In other words, you wouldn't *want* them to help,' Eric said quietly. 'Because it would mean mud flying around. And that would hurt you personally.'

Sutherland was quiet for a little while, glowering uncertainly. Then he shrugged. 'All right, I'll be straight with you, Ward. My contract as an executive director with Goldwaters carries certain share options being made available to me at the end of the year. Dependent upon performance criteria, of course. If this *Sierra Nova* thing isn't resolved quickly, there are some shareholders who might question the criteria; might even want to renege on the arrangement. I wouldn't want that to happen.' He glared at Eric suspiciously. 'I want all this kept confidential. I don't want the Edwards smuggling operation brought out in the open. At the moment the *Sierra Nova* arrest is a documentation thing, and I want it kept that way. But I think it's a bloody front for something else. There's something going on, and I want you to find out what the hell it is.'

'You think they're trying to build a case?'

'I don't know what the hell they're up to! My guess is that they're trying to link Edward's smuggling activity to Goldwaters in some way, and I won't stand for that! It's just bullshit! He was just a casual hand, for God's sake! So, you keep quiet, you use your contacts in the police and along the river, you find out just what the problem really is, and you report only to me.'

'Before the end of the month.'

'Correct.'

'That's if I agree to act for you in this matter.'

Sutherland's eyes glittered; his tone was cynical. 'I think you'll agree, all right, in view of the retainer I'm prepared to offer you.'

Chapter Two

'Things are looking up,' Susie Cartwright commented, her blue eyes widening as she looked at the Goldwaters cheque Eric had handed her for banking. 'I foresee clear skies ahead.'

'It does *not* mean you get a new computer,' Eric commented firmly. 'I don't want you getting ideas above your station. And if I'm to earn the advance retainer I've been paid, I need to get some work done. So, first of all, get hold of that court clerk who's sweet on you–'

'Mr Ward, whatever do you mean? I'm a respectable widow,' she complained archly.

'–and find out what's the position regarding a man called Edwards, arrested for suspected drug smuggling aboard a ship called the *Sierra Nova*. Find out if he's been granted bail, and when the next arraignment will be held. It will be useful to discover who is acting for Edwards, also. Ask around, sweetheart some people, bat your eyelids, pull the usual strings.'

Susie shook her head sadly. 'The things I have to do to keep this practice going...' She contemplated the cheque in quiet appreciation. Then her brow clouded. 'You're getting this for working on a drugs case?'

'Not exactly. Bit more complicated than that. Anyway, while you're getting on with that, I'd better clear my desk.'

'There's a letter in from the newspaper. About Mr Tilt.' She sniffed as she mentioned the name; Eric was aware that Joe Tilt was one of the clients of whom she did not approve, young, handsome, well dressed as he might be. She regarded his background as shady. Which it was, Eric smiled to himself. 'And Mr Tilt himself rang in also: wants to know the state of play.'

'Getting edgy, is he?'

'Sounded a bit impatient. He's at court this

33

afternoon. But not represented by you. Why do you think he'd be using other firms?'

Eric grinned. 'Spreading the load, I imagine.'

From the look she gave him, Eric knew she'd have preferred Joe Tilt taking all his business to other firms. He left her, smiling, and walked into his office. Among the papers on his desk he found the letter she had referred to. He sat down and read it carefully. It amounted to a complete withdrawal of the comments that had been made by them regarding Mr Joseph Tilt's alleged involvement in unethical practices in the restaurant trade on Tyneside.

'We are prepared as a matter of course, in making an offer of amends, to insert a statement to that effect in their next issue, and we would be prepared in addition to make a small donation to a charity of Mr Tilt's choosing, as a form of recompense. All this is offered, naturally, without prejudice.'

Eric smiled, and shook his head. Since Joe Tilt first approached him over the matter he had taken the trouble to dig a little into Tilt's background. Joe Tilt was about thirty five years old now, but he had grown up quickly from his poverty-stricken origins south of the river. From what Eric had been able to glean from his enquiries, Joe Tilt was one of those men who always managed to wriggle away from responsibilities – whether it was with women, dubious dealings, business partnerships, it was always the same. His father had been a pitman from Shiny Row, but Joe had escaped his background before he was fifteen. He'd taken advantage of the trading opportunities available along the river: scrap deals had led to second hand cars; a short period in the printing business seemed to have given him entry to other business opportunities, and the patronage of a few night club owners, members of a Wearside syndicate, had given him a further boost, and a new interest. Now, he ran a chain of restaurants in the North East, and was doing well. A young man going places – and with no criminal record on the books. But the whispers were there; Joe Tilt was not the kind of man to fall out with. Things could happen if he was crossed ... though it never seemed possible to point to his own, personal involvement in any subsequent mayhem that might occur.

On the other hand, Tilt had seemed somewhat edgy about the newspaper article, and the libel suit he had threatened, through Eric. But the newspaper had backed down remarkably quickly. Maybe there was pressure behind the scenes. Eric shrugged mentally. The fact was, the newspaper was withdrawing the allegation and that was all that Tilt seemed to want.

He dictated some letter for Susie to get typed up on the new computer. Susie slipped out to get him a sandwich for his lunch, so he was able to work on various papers on his desk throughout the lunch period. By three in the afternoon he was clear. Susie tapped on the door and came in. 'Don't forget you've got a bail application on this afternoon at three-thirty. Court number three.'

Eric grimaced. 'The breaking and entering?'

'Little scumbag,' Susie said contemptuously. 'I'd lock him away for a long time, myself. Throw away the key.'

'I'm just acting for him,' Eric protested. 'Doesn't

mean I'm on his side.'

'Even so...' She sniffed, and inspected her note-book. 'Okay, I've got what you wanted. This man Edwards that you're interested in, he's actually down for a hearing later this week. Bail was refused, and he's on remand. All seems a bit serious, with the police continuing with their enquiries.'

'Have you been able to find out who's running the case?'

She regarded him owlishly. 'Old friend of yours. DCI Spate.'

Eric felt a prickling at the back of his eyes, the first scratching of an old tension. He nodded. 'I'll have to go see him.' He did not relish the prospect. 'And who's acting for Edward's defence?'

'Archer and Samson. Mr Archer is dealing with it personally, it seems.'

Teddy Archer. Eric grimaced. He had come across Archer before – inevitably, since Archer had a considerable criminal practice on Tyneside. The firm had been established by old man Archer, but since Teddy had taken it over expansion had been swift. But Teddy Archer himself was regarded with a certain suspicion among his peers: he was aggressive and unscrupulous, and there was talk that there had been occasions when his conduct had bordered on the unethical. Even for a lawyer, Eric mused, aware that the profession had more than its share of critics. Archer had been hauled up before the Law Society a few times, reprimanded once, but no specific charges of misconduct had been brought against him. Nevertheless, there were rumours that swirled around the local law society. The man was sociable, confident, with a hail fellow well met attitude, but he was not well regarded by his peers.

'Right, that's fine. I'll have to try to get to see him. Meanwhile–'

'The bail application,' Susie said firmly.

'I'm on my way.'

It was only a short walk to the new law courts behind Wesley Square. He made his way through the security check, raising his hand in greeting to the officers on duty in the room housing the security cameras and smiled at the slim young woman on duty. 'Afternoon Mandy.'

'Hello, Mr Ward. Third floor, is it?'

'That's it.' He ignored the lift and made his way up the flights of stairs ahead of him. He passed the district judge apartments, and when he entered, Eric checked the case list. Susie had been correct: Court Three. He made his way in for his bail application hearing. It was granted quickly enough, even though Eric suspected that the young tearaway he was representing would use his time on the streets to good effect and do a bit more breaking and entering while he waited for his case to be heard, just to keep his hand in.

As he was leaving the courtroom to make his way back towards the stairs, someone tapped his shoulder. He turned to face a young woman he knew.

'Detective Constable Start.'

'Detective Sergeant, now,' Elaine Start replied.

'Congratulations. Your promotion is deserved, I'm sure.'

She ignored the compliment. 'That character you just got back onto the streets. You know he'll

37

be over the rooftops again this evening, don't you?'

'We all have a job to do,' Eric replied, turning towards the stairs as she walked beside him.

'And mine gets more difficult because of the job you do, Mr Ward. Don't you ever feel it's been like a ... crossing over?'

'I got over that feeling long ago. When I was a copper I did my job, the way you do yours. Now, I'm a lawyer. It's just a different job. And remember, I do the occasional prosecution too. When I'm instructed.'

She grinned suddenly. 'I don't think Charlie Spate is all that keen on instructing you to act for the police.'

'That's DCI Spate's loss,' Eric smiled back. He hesitated, slowing, and glanced sideways at her. 'Talking of Charlie Spate, I hear he's handling this Edwards case. The alleged drug smuggling business.'

Elaine Start observed him calmly. 'You hear right. You got an interest in Edwards? Don't tell me he's another scumbag you're going to represent.'

Eric shook his head. 'No, nothing like that. I'm involved sort of peripherally.'

'*Peripherally,* is it? I'll tell Charlie Spate that. He'll like that word, though maybe he won't know what it means.'

Eric laughed. 'I get the impression there's not much love lost between you and Spate.'

She raised an eyebrow. 'I didn't say that. In fact, I think he quite fancies me. But you want to see him, about the Edwards thing? I can tell him.'

Eric nodded. 'I'm happy to come out to Ponte-

38

land to have a word.'

'I'm sure he'll be equally happy to see you, since your interest is only *peripheral*.' She paused, as they stood just in front of the glass doors leading to the stairwell. She frowned slightly, and nodded towards the man who had just emerged from one of the witness rooms. As he made his way towards them across the blue patterned carpet of the waiting area, she muttered, 'Looks like another of your clients is heading this way. You do keep strange company, Mr Ward.'

She turned, pushed open the glass doors and made her way down the stairs. Eric glanced back and recognised the man approaching in long strides. It was Joe Tilt, quick, confident, handsome head thrusting forward aggressively. A young woman walked just behind him, carrying some heavy files. Tilt raised his hand. 'Mr Ward. The man I was hoping to see.'

'Mr Tilt. I was told you might be around here this afternoon. I have good news for you. The newspaper wants to settle.'

'They're running scared,' Tilt sneered in contempt. 'But no matter. It's small beer anyway. An irritation. I'll trust you to deal with it, as far as adequate terms are concerned. I just wanted to have a quick word, to see how things were getting along.'

Joe Tilt was only of medium height but he sparked with suppressed energy. He was dressed casually enough, in windcheater and jeans, open-necked shirt, but he gave the impression of barely controlled power, in his manner, in his quick, jerky movements, in the staccato nature of his speech.

His skin was pale, somewhat blotchy and his dark eyes were always on the move, searching, checking, weighing up opportunities, looking for an edge. He turned, aware of the young woman standing beside him. 'Seems like I'm in the company of nothing but lawyers these days. You know each other?'

Eric stared at the woman. She was about thirty, he guessed. Medium height, clear skin, frank grey eyes, an easy smile. There was something familiar about her. 'I'm not sure...'

'How unflattering,' she said lightly. 'I know you. Eric Ward, isn't it? Know about you, seen you in court—'

'Ah, of course,' Eric said, shaking his head, 'you're in—'

'Victoria Chambers. I'm Sharon Owen.'

'Of course, forgive me.' Eric did not know her in fact, though he recalled having seen her from time to time. He had never worked with her; he rarely had occasion to brief barristers from Victoria Chambers.

'Forgive you for what?' she laughed. 'We've never been introduced before. It's just that you've been around longer than I have and you know how it is – the younger ones tend to remember the older ones, rather than the other way around.'

'That puts me in the elderly pigeonhole, at least.'

'Hey, I didn't mean it like that,' she exclaimed, colouring slightly. 'I meant experience, rather than age.'

Joe Tilt raised his head, looking around at the waiting room. 'Courts make me nervous. And lawyers' chat, even more so. Anyway, Ward, there's no more problems over that newspaper article, right? Screw the bastards a bit, but don't spend too much time on it for me. And you, Miss Owen, we finished now, right?'

'I'll need another conference, maybe Thursday,' the barrister replied firmly. 'There are still some loose ends we have to tie up.'

'Yeah, sure, Thursday, we'll get together. I'll give you a ring. Okay, that's it? I'll leave you two to get on with things.'

He left them abruptly, marching off at a quick gait towards the lift. Eric watched him go, outlined against the broad windows overlooking the sunlit river and the Gateshead bank. Sharon Owen looked at Eric, raised her eyebrows and laughed. 'A man in a hurry.'

'Seems like.' Eric looked at her appraisingly. 'So you're acting for Joe Tilt as well.'

'Briefed by Archer's.'

'And what has Joe Tilt been up to?'

'Alleged interference with contracts,' she replied.

Awkwardly, she shifted the weight of the files in her arms.

'I could give you a hand with those,' Eric suggested.

'If you do, I'll buy you a coffee,' she replied. 'But not in the canteen here!'

Charlie Spate leaned back in his chair and yawned hugely. He crossed his legs, locked his hands behind his head and took a long, slow look at Elaine Start. He liked looking at Elaine: she had all the qualities he desired in a woman. Dark hair and direct eyes; good bosom, great legs. And

41

an intellect that was sharp, almost as sharp as her tongue could be. But he liked that. She didn't kowtow, she could stand up for herself – and she certainly knew how to handle men like Charlie. He sighed inwardly; maybe that was the one thing that disturbed him about her. He hadn't found a way through even the outer ring of her defences. 'So,' he said, 'I haven't had chance to congratulate you on your promotion.'

'So is this it?'

He nodded, grinning. 'It is.'

'It's nice to feel appreciated.'

'Yeah, well, appreciation continues only as long as you're doing your job.'

'Which is what I wanted to talk to you about,' she remarked firmly.

'Dissatisfied already with the rank?'

'I'm talking about the Flinders business,' she replied, ignoring the jibe. 'I've been trying to get hold of you to talk it through but you never seem to be available.'

He would have been pleased to make himself available to Elaine Start, Charlie thought to himself, but he wasn't sure she had a predilection for lean, wrong-side-of-forty coppers, and until he got the right signals he'd have to keep a tight rein on his behaviour. He'd been in trouble before, in the Met, during the Fraud Squad enquiry, and it had been the reason for his transfer north. Nothing had been proved of course, but hints about using prostitutes for services other than mere inform-ation, getting too close to some of the criminal fraternity, it had been enough to make the top brass suggest a move north might suit the interests of all. He shook his head regretfully, and sighed. 'So fill me in on it now.'

She pursed her lips. Her mouth was wide, and generous. A sexy mouth, Charlie considered. 'You'll probably remember,' she suggested, 'we got a tip off from Customs and Excise that a fleet of lorries were coming in from Zeebrugge and heading for a northern rendezvous. We agreed to mount a joint exercise. They were a bit vague at the time, and it was thought that the smuggling ring were shipping in some illegal immigrants, but it turned out to be–'

'Cigarettes.'

'That's right, sir, cigarettes. There were three lorries and we put a tail on each of them when they headed into Northumberland. But the first two lorries cottoned on to the Customs shadow and they split; unfortunately it all got a bit Wild West then–'

'A chase and a shoot-out?'

She ignored his mocking tone. Firmly, she went on, 'Two of the lorries were detained just north of Alnwick, but the third proved more difficult. We don't think the driver knew we were on his tail, but can't be sure. And the officers chasing the vehicle got maybe a bit over-excited; there was an accident–'

'And the driver ended up in hospital.'

'He died yesterday.'

There was a short silence, while Charlie Spate swore silently. This would be another rod for the Chief to break over his back. No senior officers present; charge of the bloody Light Brigade through the night; police drivers losing their cool.

43

He raised his eyes, met Elaine Start's glance. 'So, what is it you want?'

'I want to know who's in charge. *Sir.* I understood I was reporting to you, but I don't seem to be able to get hold of you. I ran the operational side, but I'm stymied. With an operation that's gone adrift, and a man dead, I need to know where I stand on this one.'

'Well, I'll tell you where you stand, Detective Sergeant. You still report to me, and keep me informed of exactly what's going on. But you started by fronting this with Customs and Excise, and that's the way it goes on. If things have been bungled, you've got to handle it. The screw-ups are down to you. And the sorting is down to you, as well.'

Her tone was cool. 'So I'm to get on with things, and carry the can if it all goes haywire. But if I sort it–'

'I'll take the credit,' he grinned maliciously. 'Aw, come on Elaine, you know the way the things work around here. What's really biting at you?'

'Delay,' she snapped. 'The Customs people don't know the ropes; they're insisting on doing the legwork on interrogations, and that's fine as far as it goes, but they don't have the experience, and they're bending the rules. Anything they do find out, well, there's the chance it would get thrown out of court as inadmissible. But I don't have the authority–'

'To do what?'

Her eyes glinted. 'To take steps to pin down the people behind this scam.'

'You got any leads?' Charlie asked, interested.

'There's word along the river. I'd like to follow it up. But while you're in charge...'

'Nominal charge,' Charlie sighed. He would have quite liked to go skulking along the alleyways on Tyneside with Elaine Start: the old days on the street had been good. But he had other matters to attend to now, under the Deputy Chief Constable's thumb. 'Look, as far as I'm concerned you've got *carte blanche* to follow your instincts. Those wet-nurses in Customs don't know their arses from their elbows and I've no doubt they'll blow it when they come to the interrogations. So you stay clear of that. But now, with this guy dead–'

'Flinders,' she interrupted impatiently. 'He was called Flinders.'

'Whatever. Now he's gone feet up we've got to go carefully. Will the media scream police negligence?'

'They're almost bound to. It's the way they sell papers.'

'Then it's important we put the finger on the racket and keep it there, until we can put someone away. It diverts attention. So you do just that. Follow your leads. Divert attention.'

'And the politics?'

Charlie grimaced. 'That's why I'm here. In charge. I'll deal with the flak: you get the results.'

She regarded him quizzically, not displeased with what she was hearing. 'Just what exactly is keeping you off this enquiry, sir?'

Charlie gritted his teeth. 'Liaison,' he muttered. 'Keeping the Deputy Chief Constable happy in his relationships with other operations.'

45

'Vague.'

'Politics.'

'All to do with the *Sierra Nova?*'

Charlie Spate's eyes narrowed as he stared at the young woman in front of him. 'What's the scuttlebutt doing the rounds?' he asked curiously.

She shrugged. 'People have been asking why a DCI is spending so much time on a scumbag operation, the arrest of a guy who's been caught smuggling drugs off a freighter. And why the ship he was on – the *Sierra Nova* – has been arrested when there's seemingly no suggestion that the smuggler was anything other than small time, a one man band. And just why the hell no one seems to be talking about any of it.'

The bloody Deputy Chief Constable and his bloody restrictions, Charlie swore under his breath. 'So there's talk around the canteen.'

She nodded. 'And elsewhere. And Eric Ward would like to see you.'

'So?'

'About this very thing.'

'The *Sierra Nova?*' Charlie crinkled his brow. Now that was interesting. 'I wonder what the *Sierra Nova* has to do with a crappy practice on the Quayside.'

'If you meet him, you'll find out,' Elaine Start replied. 'Meanwhile, I'll get on with my job, now I've got your clearance.'

'But you'll report,' Charlie snarled meaningfully.

She gave him a sweet smile. 'Of course, DCI Spate. After all, you are in charge.'

Too smart, too tart, Charlie considered, but she gave him a tingle where she shouldn't. He'd have to do something about that one of these days, he knew it. But he'd have to tread carefully, make sure of his ground. And meanwhile, there was the solicitor Eric Ward. And the small matter of the Deputy Chief Constable and the detained freighter, sailing under the name *Sierra Nova...*

Chapter Three

Anne was looking good. True, she seemed a little thinner, and there was a certain nervous tension in her manner, but there was a sparkle of determination in her eyes as she sat beside her lawyer, John Elkins, in the well appointed Westgate office which displayed a marked contrast with Eric's own. Eric took the seat offered him as Elkins shuffled the papers on his desk, glanced briefly at Anne and cleared his throat nervously.

'I've asked you here, Mr Ward, to discuss some of the detailed proposals that Mrs Ward has made. There was, of course, no prenuptial settlement but my client feels that it is only appropriate that the contribution you made to the marriage during the years should be properly recognised and compensated for. Accordingly, as you will see from the documents placed before you we have taken account of the work you did on behalf of Mrs Ward as a director of Martin and Channing–'

'I received director's fees for that work,' Eric interrupted. 'They were adequate and commensurate with my efforts. There is no need to discuss further … compensation.' His eyes met Anne's; she stared at him defiantly for a long moment, then looked away.

Elkins's bald head gleamed as he leaned forward; he adjusted his glasses and chewed at his lip. 'You don't seem to understand, Mr Ward. These proposals are very much to your advantage. I have already advised Mrs Ward that she does not need to demonstrate such generosity–'

'No, it's you who does not seem to understand,' Eric interrupted calmly. 'I have resisted this meeting, but in the end I thought it best to appear, in order that I make my feelings clear. I want no compensation for a failed marriage. I want nothing from the estate left to Anne by her father; I want nothing from Sedleigh Hall; I want nothing from the considerable development of the business interests she has undertaken. She has other advisers now; I want nothing, other than the items I have already written to you about.'

Elkins scratched at his cheek in irritated indecision. 'The flat in Gosforth is already in your name, and though I've suggested it should be brought into the marriage settlement, my client is not of that opinion. But … so be it. But you should be warned, Mr Ward, that if you resist this settlement, there will be no opportunity later to dispute the sharing of marital assets after the final decree absolute is issued. Moreover…'

Eric held up his hand, silencing the frowning lawyer seated beside his wife. 'Just hold it there. I've already made it abundantly clear that I shall make no claim against my wife's assets, now or in the future. The flat was bought by me, from my own earnings, though it was used by both of us. Sedleigh Hall, the Morcomb estates in Northumberland, everything else is Anne's. I've no desire to disturb that: now we've agreed that divorce is the best option open to us, I want to take away nothing other than the few personal items I've designated.'

'But that's not fair!' Anne protested angrily. 'Why are you being so stupid, and so stubborn? You played a major part in the development of my business, you know that! And the work you did while at Martin and Channing, I couldn't have managed without you. Why do you insist on behaving this way, leaving me in debt to you–'

Eric leaned back in his chair, shaking his head sadly. 'It's not a question of debt, Anne. We had a good marriage. The reasons for its ending we needn't go into now. But I've always made it clear to you where I stand.'

'Your ridiculous independence!' she burst out.

'Stupid, stubborn, ridiculous, it doesn't matter how you want to describe it,' he replied quietly. 'I married you for what you were, not what you had. And while we were married I went my own way, lived my own professional life–'

'In that puerile, limited practice on the Quayside,' she exclaimed bitterly.

'It was my practice,' he rejoined. 'My professional life. It was what I wanted to do; what I was good at.'

'But there could have been so much more.'

'I didn't want it. Not then. And not now.'

There was a short silence. Elkins shuffled in his seat. This was clearly a situation he was unused to dealing with; Eric himself admitted it was rather unusual. But he meant what he said. The marriage was grinding to its close. He wanted no bitterness in their separation. And he wanted nothing from the marriage that he did not believe he had earned – and not even that.

Anne was glaring at him in frustration; he sensed she was near to tears. He did not want that. 'Look, Anne, I've got the flat, I've got my practice, I've got my life.'

'But how will you manage?' she insisted.

'As I've always done. By my own efforts.'

Elkins glanced helplessly at his client, and shrugged. 'It seems to me, Mrs Ward, that there's nothing more I can do. If Mr Ward is insistent–'

'He is,' Eric interrupted firmly.

'Then I think I should draw up the documents in the manner suggested in the first instance by Mr Ward, get them signed by both parties, properly witnessed ... and leave it at that.'

Eric stood up, nodding. Anne rose also, biting her lip in defeat. 'I'm not happy about this, Eric.'

'I can't say I'm happy about *any* of it,' he replied.

She hesitated, uncertain. 'I know you well enough to realise you won't change your mind over this ... stupid stance of yours. And I know you'll never come to me for help, even if you needed it.' She managed a smile, somewhat tremulous at the corners. 'You'll look after yourself, won't you?'

'Haven't I always?' he asked, and kissed her goodbye.

When he got back to the office Susie left him alone at his desk for a while, sensing that he was preoccupied after the meeting with his wife. It was late afternoon when she tapped on the door and came in. 'I thought you'd like to know, that young tearaway you got bail for, he was arrested again last night. Breaking and entering. He wants you to represent him.'

Eric groaned. 'Not again. I can't think of anything new to say.'

'Neither can I. I've said it all before. But you won't listen. So I've given up.' She hesitated, reluctant to interfere. 'Your meeting with Mrs Ward ... was it rough?'

Eric looked at her, smiled despondently. 'No, not really. It's just that Anne can't seem to grasp I want nothing from her.'

'Oh, I'm sure she knows that,' Susie contradicted. 'The reality is, she wants to help you in spite of your stubbornness. One way of looking at things is to suggest you're placing a burden of guilt on her shoulders, and maybe she feels that's not fair. She walks away with all she holds, and you're left with nothing.'

'You sound as though you're on her side,' Eric growled suspiciously.

'I am, in some things.' She took a deep breath, brushed back an errant lock of hair with a determined hand. 'It's all very well, asserting your independence. But can't you see, even in a situation like this, such assertion can hurt?'

'I can't help being who I am, Susie,' he said after a short silence.

'Oh, I know that. And I never thought you'd be made to change. But that doesn't mean I'm not entitled to speak my mind.'

51

'I could sack you,' he said in irritation.

'But you wouldn't. Not for a reason like that – speaking my mind. I know that well enough too.' She giggled nervously. 'Wouldn't have said it otherwise. So what are you going to do now? Do a big strong male Achilles, and sulk in your tent?'

'I've got work to finish up here. Then, maybe later–'

'Maybe later you'll do what you promised to do, and attend that charity function at the Gosforth Park Hotel.'

Eric groaned aloud. 'Oh hell, I'd forgotten about that. I don't think I'm really in the mood...'

'No skulking, Mr Ward,' she said firmly. 'Tonight, you're on the town. On your own. Maybe time to howl a bit.'

'Among a bunch of fusty lawyers and businessmen?' Eric grinned. 'I hardly think so.'

Thankfully, Anne was not present at the charity dinner. He had half expected that she might be there, but guessed that she would have noted the guest list and decided that it would not be appropriate in the circumstances. So he was spared the anxiety of meeting her there in company with Jason Sullivan, legal adviser and probable lover, and he was able to relax, try to avoid the gnawing that persisted in his heart and mind, and make an appearance of enjoying himself. So he ate, made polite social conversation with those seated near him, drank a few glasses of wine, and danced once or twice with safe, matronly acquaintances who were a little too keen to be sympathetic, until gradually he became more and more depressed. Finally, he made his way to the bar and ordered a stiff whisky, seated on the stool, staring blindly into the mirror behind the bar and contemplating what a mess he had made of his life to date.

Several drinks later, he felt a hand slap his shoulder. 'Ward! Long face, on a joyous occasion? Have another drink my friend, and the world will seem a better place!'

Teddy Archer was of medium height, bland features and thinning, reddish hair. He was about forty now, had been divorced several years ago, worked out regularly to keep a trim figure and tended to escort younger women to functions like this. He had a young woman beside him now. It was Sharon Owen.

'You've met Sharon, of course. What'll it be, Ward? Whisky? Another double, hey?' He slapped Eric on the shoulder again, and winked at Sharon. He failed to keep the underlying, mocking malice out of his tones. 'We go way back, Ward and me. Seen a few villains put away – with the help of the Bar of course,' he leered. 'But there's one thing in which we've always differed. Ward here, he despises the high life, isn't interested in wealthy clients – not even his wife – and wants to muck around in the mud along the Tyne. But there's room for all sorts, isn't that right? Somebody's got to do the dirty work, deal with the mucky ones. I'm just glad it doesn't have to be me! I never was turned on by scrabbling around with the river rats.'

Eric had never liked Archer. Now, a sudden anger grabbed at him. It might have been the effect of the drink he had consumed, his earlier meeting with Anne, or of his general depression, but he suddenly knew that he wanted to plant a fist in Teddy Archer's smug, vacuous face, and wipe off the vicious corners of his smile. He slid off the stool, bunching his fist. Perhaps Archer saw it coming; he gasped, stepped back a little, and then Sharon Owen was inserting herself between the two men, gracefully, determinedly. She put a hand on Eric's arm. 'I'm glad I've caught up with you, Mr Ward.'

He stared at her uncomprehendingly, the blood still stirring angrily in his veins.

'The matter we discussed over coffee the other day,' she went on. 'I've had further thoughts about it. Perhaps we could have a word now?' She turned, smiled sweetly at the solicitor who had led her to the bar. 'You won't mind, will you Teddy? Perhaps you could send my drink – and Mr Ward's – over to that table there. We'll need to have a private talk for a while.'

Archer, somewhat flushed and panicky, was nettled, but indecisive. He glanced from Eric to the girl and was clearly unhappy at losing his prize. 'Maybe we can get together later,' he muttered.

'Maybe,' she replied, her tone making no commitment.

She took Eric's arm and propelled him firmly away from the bar to the table in the corner. Briskly, she took the two empty glasses from the table and took them back to the bar. When she returned Eric had sat down, and most of his anger had dissipated. He managed a rueful smile. 'I suppose I have to thank you. I was about to make a complete fool of myself.'

'If there are thanks to be handed out, I think

Teddy Archer ought to be thanking me,' she smiled. 'I had the distinct impression you were about to lay him out, and I don't think he'd have been able to retaliate. And, also ... I have to thank you.'

'For what?'

'For giving me the chance to dump the creep. He's been trying to grab my knee under the table all through dinner.'

'Trying?'

'He got a few fork prong marks for his trouble, in the back of his hand. But he stayed persistent. Pawed me on the dance floor, dragged me to the bar for a drink, and has been angling to take me home afterwards ... what's a girl to do but grin and bear it? Young barristers need to keep briefing solicitors reasonably happy.'

He smiled at her. 'From what I hear, it's forensic skill rather than a shapely knee that brings you your briefs.'

'Now that sounds like a compliment. And that looks like a smile. You feeling somewhat better now?'

Eric took a deep breath, and nodded. A waiter approached them, placed two drinks in front of them and stated that they were with Mr Archer's compliments. Sharon Owen giggled and raised her glass. 'Here's to Teddy Archer, then.'

Eric looked around, to see the disconsolate figure of the solicitor making his way back to the dance floor. He sipped his drink, looked at the young barrister beside him. Her hair was swept up, carefully arranged; her eyes were friendly; her bare shoulders gleamed against the dark blue of her dress and he could see the first hint of the swell of her breasts. He could understand why Teddy Archer had been making a play for Sharon Owen.

'So, you approve of what you see?'

Eric laughed. 'I'm sorry for staring. But yes, I do. Good Samaritans rarely come so beautiful.'

'I was taking advantage of the situation for my own reasons,' she warned. 'I wasn't just feeling sorry for you.' She hesitated. 'You seemed to be doing pretty well on that front for yourself. Bad day?'

'Bad enough,' Eric admitted. He didn't want to dwell on the thought, and asked, 'So what was it you wanted to discuss with me?'

They had had coffee together briefly, a few days earlier, and had talked in generalities but he had no recollection of any unfinished matters.

'That was just an excuse,' Sharon replied, twirling her glass between her fingers. 'I could just see trouble coming between you and Archer, and stepped in. No, nothing really to discuss, other than, maybe a mutual client of ours.'

'Be careful of legal privilege,' he warned.

'Between lawyers?' She laughed. He liked the sound. 'No, I was just wondering what you thought of Joe Tilt.'

Eric grimaced. 'I don't know a great deal about him. It's well enough known that he's from a rough background, has done well enough for himself on the relatively shady side of the street, and has no criminal record.'

'You've settled his libel suit for him.'

'That's right. And you?'

56

She pouted a little; it was measured, but attractive. 'Well, things are progressing, but not all that well. The other side – Northern Food Supplies – are pressing hard on the interference with contracts issue. A Manchester firm, but they've tied up most of the north east in supplies deliveries. They're claiming that Joe Tilt has used ... undue pressure on some of their existing clients to break contractual arrangements of long standing.'

'Are they claiming he's used strong arm tactics?'

She allowed a frown to mar her features. 'I don't think I should talk about that ... even to another lawyer. But there are claims of ... certain irregularities. And in the papers I've been given there's some information that doesn't seem quite to fit. In fact, I'm a bit puzzled about it ... but that's my problem.'

'The Northern Foods people ... they're going to the wire on it?'

'It looks like. And I ... well, I've got a funny feeling about it. Teddy Archer gave us the brief, and I'm saddled with it, but I get the vague feeling there's more to it than is landing on my desk. And as I said, there's a few unconnected things in the files that I don't quite understand... But I hear that you've been around a while, worked as a copper, know a lot of people, so I just wondered whether you'd have any thoughts about Mr Tilt, any suggestions you could make...'

'So you want to use me, rather than rescue me?' Eric suggested mockingly.

'Hah!' she gestured at him in irritation. 'It's not like that. Anyway, forget I even asked you. Let's drink up to the confoundment of the Teddy

Archers of this world, and celebrate.' She caught something in his glance then, and she leaned forward, frowning. 'I'm sorry. Suggesting a celebration was crass. I've heard you're...'

She fell silent. He finished the thought for her. 'Getting divorced. That's right. That's the size of it.'

'It's ... difficult?'

He shrugged. 'Well, no, not really. I mean, there's no great bitterness, or animosity. The parting is relatively amicable. We had a good marriage but, it was as much my fault as hers that we sort of drifted apart, and there were a few incidents, misunderstandings ... and I suppose once the trust goes out of a marriage, it's difficult to hold the relationship together. I even believe now there was a certain inevitability about it, being the personalities we are. My obsessions were of the kind she would never understand...'

'Your practice, you mean?' Sharon asked quietly. 'It's common gossip, you could have done much better for yourself if you'd used the opportunities her circle would have given you.'

'But it wouldn't have been better for *myself*, don't you understand that?' Eric said fiercely. 'I feel there's a purpose to what I do, even if a lot of it is connected with helpless people, down and outs, the underprivileged and the weak. No, it's not lucrative, and it doesn't bring me a big office, but it's where I came from, you know that Sharon? I've dabbled with the big firms, I've worked in the boardrooms with their slick, shiny, businessmen, and I don't like it or want it. I started as a copper, and got to know Tyneside.

Getting too far away from it makes me ... uneasy.'

He sipped his drink, and glowered at the table. He suddenly saw himself as others must see him; his rationalising of his condition would never escape the fact that he grubbed out an existence on the Quayside when he could have done good work at higher levels, kept a wife who loved him, built a marriage and a life of some consequence, instead of wallowing in self pity and whisky. The thought embittered him, and suddenly the alcohol began to work its way also; he could feel the first intimations of the pain he dreaded, the scratching at the back of his eyeballs, the excruciating tearing at his nerve ends. He frowned, put the heels of his hands to his eyes and muttered to himself.

'Are you all right?' Sharon asked, leaning forward to touch his arm gently. There was concern in her voice. He forced himself to exude an element of cheerfulness. 'Yes, of course, it's just too much drink I suppose. And an exciting evening. I think I'll call it a night.' He rose, half stumbling to his feet. 'I'm sorry for this ... walking away. And I really am grateful for your stopping me making a fool of myself. I'm sure I'll see you again soon, maybe at the courts...'

He left the bar with the pain stabbing at his eyes, made his way almost blindly to the cloakroom, cursing that he had left his medication in his topcoat. He collected his coat, bent over the cloakroom washbasin and used the eye dropper to take some of the pilocarpine he always carried for emergencies. Then he waited, while the room spun, and the scratching claws extended, then slowly retracted and died. In a little while he

59

walked unsteadily to the entrance of the hotel.

Sharon Owen was standing there, waiting for him, coat over her arm. 'I've called you a cab,' she said.

She insisted on getting in with him. It was only three miles to his apartment. She asked the cab to wait while she got out and entered the building with him. Dizzy with the receding pain and the affects of unusual amounts of alcohol Eric made little protest. When he fumbled with his keys she took them from him, opened the door, led the way inside, flicking on the lights. She looked around briefly, approvingly, then turned to him. 'You sure you're going to be all right now?'

Shamefaced, he nodded. 'Role reversal, looks like. Me having a woman see me home.'

'A lot of people think I'm too pushy.'

'You've been helpful ... to a man in trouble.'

She was silent for a moment, regarding him gravely. 'When will your decree absolute be through?' she asked unexpectedly.

Surprised, he shrugged. 'Couple of weeks.'

'You still love her, don't you?'

He stared at her, but made no reply. She stepped past him after a moment, stood in the doorway, then put a hand on his shoulder. She smiled at him, and kissed him lightly on the cheek. 'I think your wife must be a very foolish woman.'

Then she was gone, the door closing quietly behind her and he was left to the spreading loneliness of the room.

Chapter Four

During the next few days Eric kept himself busy. There was the young burglar to represent; Eric did it with little conviction, in view of the villain's record, before an unsympathetic magistrate and a police solicitor who aggressively resisted further bail. There were two cases to be dealt with involving benefits frauds – a Nigerian couple who had claimed supplementary benefits payments in the names of other people by obtaining birth certificates of children who had died. There was a custodial sentence for a young hooligan who had caused death by dangerous driving, and a heavy fine for a second hand car dealer who had been 'clocking' cars with false mileages. And he was in court to hear a client of his being sentenced to eight months imprisonment with a four thousand pound fine for possessing a small quantity of cocaine, albeit claimed for his personal use only. The parade of minor villainy that was passing through his office was depressing.

The cocaine case reminded Eric of the fact that he had not yet managed to talk to DCI Charlie Spate with regard to his Goldwater retainer. Back in his office, Eric was still feeling despondent. He found himself wondering again whether Anne was indeed right, and whether the general view, mentioned to him by Sharon Owen, that maybe he was wasting his life and his talents with the low life clients that stepped regularly into his office, was correct. As for the failure of his marriage – in a sense he could come to terms with that, could rationalise what had happened with his own growing jealousy of the way Anne and Jason Sullivan had become closer over the last year. After all, Sullivan was able to show Anne the professional commitment Eric was unwilling to expose himself to. It had perhaps been the inevitable result of his own indifference, and her growing reliance on Sullivan. But it all really came back to his own fierce sense of independence. He thought of the meretricious nature of the words in the Sinatra song *My Way;* he considered how some might suggest they applied to him, and he groaned mentally.

But dwelling on such issues was foolish. He picked up the phone, asked Susie to place a call to Ponteland: he wanted to speak to DCI Spate. A few minutes later the phone rang. It was Charlie Spate.

'Mr Ward. You wanted to speak to me.'

'DCI Spate. Yes, there's something I'd like to discuss with you; a matter raised by one of my clients.'

'This would be what Elaine Start mentioned to me. The *Sierra Nova.*'

Eric hesitated. 'Well, yes, the freighter, and the reasons why it's being detained.'

There was a short silence. At last, Charlie Spate said, 'Well, as it happens there's a hearing this afternoon, concerning the man we arrested for possession on board the freighter. Sammy Edwards. I shall be at the court. Maybe we could meet after the hearing, grab a coffee together, and you can tell me what you want.'

'Nothing more than a little information, really,' Eric said carefully.

'Then who knows? Maybe we can do a trade.' There was an evil edge to his chuckle. 'Though as I recall, you still owe me, don't you?'

Eric gritted his teeth. It was just like Spate to remind him there had been an occasion when Spate had chosen not to expose Eric to professional disaster. Eric knew that one of these days Charlie Spate would call in that debt, and he had no doubt he would find the experience an unpleasant one.

'So what do you think?' Spate asked cheerfully. 'A social chat after we deal with Sammy Edwards?'

'I'll be there, outside the courtroom,' Eric agreed.

He had no appetite for lunch, as he thought over the events that had earlier led to his involvement a year ago with the death of a call girl, the debt owed to Charlie Spate, and the corrosive effect those events had had on his marriage. Everything suddenly seemed to be conspiring to underscore the way his life had gone off the rails during this last year. He tried to concentrate on the paperwork in front of him but he found it difficult. Eventually, he gave up and left the office, Susie eyeing him silently, asking no questions as he went.

The early afternoon sun was weak, the Tyne glinted blackly, the cool breeze was at his back as he walked along the Quayside, made his way up Dog Leap Stairs and idly watched the traffic thundering over the Tyne Bridge for a little while.

He walked up the hill past St Nicholas Cathedral towards what had been the ancient street markets – Cloth Market, Groat Market – and then back down, aimlessly, turning in at Amen Corner to saunter in the quieter atmosphere of the grounds beyond All Saints Church with its unique elliptical nave and galleried interior, no longer used for ecclesiastic services. From there he could catch glimpses of the river below the steep bluff, and hear the mournful calling of distant river traffic down beyond the swing of the Tyne, silvering down to Tynemouth and North Shields.

He stood there on the hill for a while, pulling himself together, getting his whirling thoughts in order. What was done, was past. He had to concentrate on the future, build up his life again and put the old mistakes behind him. And that meant, first of all, earning the retainer he had obtained from Paul Sutherland, at Goldwater & Sons. He went back down the steep steps to the Quayside, strode past the eighteenth century Customs House and the Victorian shipping offices that had denoted the vigorous maritime trade of earlier years, and proceeded towards the spectacular sandstone and glittering glass frontage of the new law courts.

Mandy was on duty again at the security check. As he stepped through the checkpoint, she said, 'Bit of a crowd in today Mr Ward.'

'Why's that?'

'Japanese tourists. Bein' given a tour of British justice on Tyneside.' She rolled her eyes. 'Why do you reckon they keep bowin', like?'

'Respect for your uniform,' he suggested, smiling, and made his way towards the stairs. He wandered along the waiting room area, for a few minutes, checking which court room was being used for the Edwards hearing. A subdued chattering came from the group of tourists, lined against the windows, busy taking photographs of the river, and the bridges and the Baltic Flour Mills building being refurbished on the Gateshead landing. A somewhat harrassed guide was talking to the duty officer seated on one of the blue benches nearby. Various other people, witnesses, friends, family supporters lounged in the waiting area, some of them commenting on the chattering group of tourists, grinning at their enthusiasm.

A few minutes later, as the Japanese group was beginning to drift away from the windows to congregate near the doors, Eric caught sight of Charlie Spate emerging from the court room in company with another man; Spate saw him, acknowledged him with a brief gesture that clearly suggested he would be available shortly, and then disappeared into one of the witness rooms, in deep conversation with the burly, short-haired man accompanying him. Eric hesitated, not sure what to do, but guessed that Spate would not be long so decided to stay where he was.

It was only a few minutes later, just as the court room door opened and the small group of men came out, that a woman started screaming abuse.

Eric was unable to make out quite what was happening. She was standing near the glass doors leading to the stairs; her voice was raised high, and a torrent of obscenities poured from her lips. The tourist guide stepped back as the duty officer rose quickly from his seat and hurried towards her. He grabbed her arm and she threw it off, screaming something unintelligible at him. For a few moments Eric stayed where he was but then he moved closer as to his left the small knot of people gathered around, and some of the Japanese tourists hurried forward, cameras at the ready, eager to photograph anything out of the ordinary. The duty security officer was now holding the woman, propelling her firmly towards the doors. Eric caught a glimpse of her: a spitting, cursing woman of dowdy, unkempt appearance. There was something familiar about her; she glared at him with wild eyes as she was dragged, still screaming abuse past Eric, bundled by the security officer through the doors and on towards the stairs to the ground floor.

But behind him further shouting had broken out, a woman screamed a warning and pandemonium ensued. The abusive woman at the entrance was disappearing down the stairs, the duty officer was staring back into the waiting area, undecided whether to make sure she had left the premises, or whether to return to the new disturbance. People were shouting, some women were running, panicked, towards the glass doors and the Japanese tourists were milling in agonised confusion. The duty officer came running back into the waiting area and towards the source of the disturbance. Eric stood undecided at the edge of the milling knot of people as some walked away hurriedly. Then he caught a brief glimpse of a huddle of people, men kneeling over someone lying on the ground, a splash of red on the white shirt of a security officer, and to one side others attending to a woman slumped against the wall of the witness room. All was confusion and noise and flashbulbs, clicking cameras, chattering and excitement. Eric heard running feet behind him; he turned and saw Charlie Spate barging his way through the milling group. He was red-faced and angry. He stopped when he reached the group huddled over the prostrate body. He grabbed a shoulder, pulled a man away. Then he snarled an obscenity, started yelling for the area to be cleared.

But Eric was staring at the woman slumped against the wall. She was being half supported by a policeman. There was blood on her head, trickling down her face.

It was Sharon Owen.

Chapter Five

The phone jangled insistently on Eric's desk. He pushed his paperwork aside with a sigh and picked it up.

'Mr Sutherland from Goldwaters is on the line,' Susie said.

Eric hesitated. 'Put him through.'

Sutherland spent no time in preliminaries. 'Have you anything to report on the *Sierra Nova?*'

'I'm afraid not yet. But I have a meeting scheduled in the next half hour, after which I hope I'll be able to have some information.'

'You're aware this thing is getting bloody

urgent, Ward.' Sutherland's tone was sharp. 'I don't want any dragging of feet. If you can't come up with what we need I'll have to seek assistance elsewhere.'

'I'll be in touch as soon as I can,' Eric replied, half wishing Sutherland would indeed go elsewhere. He disliked the man's tone and attitude. 'I want action, Ward. Like now!' Sutherland slammed down the phone without further comment.

Eric leaned back in his chair, a tingling of irritation in his veins. He had not been able to have the discussion he had planned with Charlie Spate; in the confusion of the previous day Spate had cleared the waiting area and Eric had realised that their scheduled meeting would have to be put off. The crowd had not been allowed to leave the law courts building immediately, but had been held in the entrance for a while but while names and addresses had been taken they were then allowed to leave. The morning newspapers had, naturally, headlined the sensational events at the law courts: they reported that a man called Edwards, charged with cocaine smuggling, had been knifed as he was being escorted from his hearing, and eye witnesses were quoted as having been confused by the noise and turmoil, as first an unknown, abusive woman had been ejected from the hallway, and then Edwards had been attacked. It seemed his lungs had been punctured by a single stab wound and he had died shortly after admission to the hospital. Eric knew that Charlie Spate had been involved with the Edwards case, and would presumably now have his hands full. So he was somewhat surprised when early that morning, shortly after he had got into his office, there had been a call to say that DCI Spate would be visiting him at midday. It seemed Charlie Spate was prepared to discuss the *Sierra Nova* with Eric in spite of the killing of the man in police custody.

Eric's thoughts drifted back to Sharon Owen. He had recognised her, slumped injured against the wall of the waiting area, but was unable to lend any assistance since the security guards had cleared the whole area and he had been forced to leave. He had placed a call to Victoria Chambers the next morning, however, and had been told by the clerk that Sharon had been taken to hospital with concussion, and was being kept in under observation, but would probably be well enough to return to work in a few days. Eric decided to send some flowers to her bedside, and perhaps visit her after he had completed his interview with Charlie Spate. But he was puzzled as to what exactly had happened: the newspaper account was vague. The reporter stated that a bystander had been injured but gave no other details. They had been able to provide a few photographs of the scene however, presumably culled from the clicking cameras of the Japanese tourists. Eric did not appear on any of them, but there was one clear shot of the head and shoulders of the dying man. For once, the prurience of the camera operator might be of assistance, rather than an irritation, Eric mused.

Charlie Spate was punctual, arriving at Eric's office exactly at midday, but he was not alone.

'This is Chris Michaels,' Spate announced as

they were shown into the room by Susie. 'I thought it would be useful if he came along.'

Eric shook hands with the tanned, crew-cut, broad-shouldered man in the formal dark suit: he recognised him as the person Spate had been in discussion with at the law courts the previous day. He gestured the two men to seats in front of him as he sat behind his desk. 'Susie, can you arrange for coffees for us all?' He fixed Charlie with a sharp glance. 'I'm pleased you've been able to find time to call here, after that business at the law courts. I gather from the newspaper reports that the man who was stabbed has died.'

'Absolute bloody shambles,' Charlie Spate snarled, and nodded; Chris Michaels shifted uneasily in his seat. His blue eyes were cold, his gaze steady as he observed Eric, seeming to weigh him up, making some unknown calculations. 'It was like a bloody circus there, you know what I mean? All we needed to top it was some flaming trapeze artists. I never seen anything like it! Gawkers everywhere, and security officers running around like headless chickens until our people arrived! He died in hospital,' Spate confirmed bitterly. 'You know he was the man we had arrested on a drug smuggling charge? I thought maybe he would be someone you'd want to talk to me about.'

Eric shook his head. 'Me? No ... at least not directly... But what exactly happened there at the courts?'

Charlie Spate's eyes were evasive. He glanced at his companion, twisted his mouth in uncertainty, and shrugged. 'The matter is still under investigation, of course, so I don't want to say too much. You'll probably be contacted later today to give your own statement. It's been bedlam: we had to talk to everyone who was there, including the Nips, and you can imagine what mayhem that caused! They have security cameras operating in the public areas of the building, and you wouldn't believe it but they don't take copies of what's going on! The cameras are there just to alert security down below, in case there's any trouble. On the other hand, there was one good thing about having those Japs there ... a couple of them were using video cameras so we've got some footage of the scene. It means we should be able to identify individuals, and work out exactly what happened.' He cocked his head to one side, inquisitively. 'Just exactly what did *you* see? You weren't too far from the action.'

Eric considered his reply for a moment. 'I don't know... It was all somewhat confusing. I was waiting for you outside the witness room, as you know–' He glanced at Michaels, but the man's features were impassive. Eric wondered who he represented, and exactly why he was here. 'I suppose the first thing I noticed was the shouting and screaming ... some woman was yelling abuse, and was shown the stairs, ordered out of the building.'

'Yeah, they have just the one security officer on duty on each floor,' Spate announced in disgust. 'The guy didn't see her out of course – he came back into the waiting area once he sent her off on the stairs. And by the time she got downstairs, they didn't pay much attention as she left, because of the mayhem going on up above. They were clustered around the screen, and calling for police backup. What a bloody shambles... You get a good look at her?' Spate asked.

Eric nodded. 'Yes ... and she looked familiar. I have a feeling I know her, but I'm not sure.'

There was a short silence, while the two men stared at him expectantly. Spate spoke to Michaels at last, as though in explanation. 'Mr Ward used to be a copper. There's things he learned on his Tyneside beat.' He turned back to Eric. 'Is that how you came across this woman? Was it from the old days?'

Eric shrugged. 'I'm not sure. I'll have to think about it. You believe she was involved in this killing?'

'We're keeping all our lines open. We'd certainly like to talk to her. So, if you do recall the name, or anything else about her, be sure to let me know. So ... what then?'

'As I say, it was all a bit confused. The noise, the woman being ejected...' Eric frowned. 'Then there was another commotion, just outside the court-room door. A lot of people rushing about, and the Japanese group milling around in excitement. I went forward, saw ... Edwards it was, I suppose, lying on the ground. One of his security escorts with him, blood on his white shirt... They didn't appear to be regular policemen...' He waited, but Spate's features were like stone. 'And then I recognised Sharon Owen. What exactly happened there?'

'Owen. The barrister,' Charlie Spate grimaced. 'I thought you might know her. Too early to get a clear reconstruction, really. It seems she just got caught up in the general mayhem. She got knocked sideways, struck her head against the wall. She doesn't remember much about anything that happened.'

'You've already interviewed Sharon Owen in hospital?' Eric asked.

There must have been some implied criticism in his voice for Charlie Spate's tone hardened. 'Look, this is a murder enquiry Ward. You know what happens in cases like this – all the stops get pulled out. And like I told you, first thing is we have to talk to all the potential witnesses – including those damned tourists – so we can't hang around just because some young woman got in the way and had her head thumped by accident.'

They were interrupted by a light tap on the door, and Susie came in with a tray holding three coffees. She handed them around, her glance flicking towards Eric as she became aware of the cold silence in the room. She left, closing the door quietly behind her.

'I gather Sharon's concussed,' Eric said firmly. 'In such a situation–'

'We should pussyfoot around?' Charlie Spate sneered, reached for one of the coffee cups and sipped at it. 'We have had a word with her but she doesn't remember much. Maybe when she's clear again she'll remember something more, but we can't wait around.' He eyed Eric suspiciously. 'Just how well do you know her?'

Eric bristled somewhat. He met Spate's gaze levelly. 'We've met a few times. That's all.'

There was deliberate, goading malice in Spate's tone. 'I just wondered for a moment whether you were jumping from one bed into another.'

Eric sat very still, hands clenched below the top of his desk. The atmosphere had been cool earlier but now it was chilly with hostility. He took a deep breath, aware that something was needling Spate, and that in some curious way Spate was venting his anger on the man facing him, striking out almost blindly, rather than directing it at its source. Eric had the suspicion that he was not the real target for Spate's anger, but the words had nevertheless been offensive. He kept his temper in check. 'No, nothing like that. As I've already said, I know her only slightly. She has a good reputation at the local Bar; I've never briefed her personally, and I've met her socially, once or twice – most recently the other evening, at a charity dinner.'

There was a short silence as Charlie Spate glowered at him. Chris Michaels leaned forward. 'I don't believe, Mr Ward, that you wanted to talk to Mr Spate about Sharon Owen,' he said quietly. There was the hint of an Australian accent in his placatory tone.

Eric noted the spasm of anger that touched Charlie Spate's mouth, at the goading interruption. It interested him. He nodded. 'That's right. I wanted to discuss the seizure of the freighter called the *Sierra Nova*.'

'And just exactly what did you want to know about it?' Michaels went on, as Spate stirred in his chair.

'I understand,' Eric replied slowly, 'that the ship has been arrested and held, prevented from leaving port, with a number of charges pending. I was aware that this man who was killed yesterday – Edwards – had also been held on a charge of

74

smuggling drugs. I was going to ask Mr Spate whether there was any connection between the Edwards matter, and the detaining of the freighter.'

'None.' The word was almost spat out by Spate.

Michaels ignored him. He folded his muscular arms, gazed at Eric reflectively. 'Just precisely what is your interest in the *Sierra Nova*, Mr Ward?'

Eric raised an eyebrow. 'Clearly, no personal interest. But I am under instruction from my clients.'

'Would they be the owners of the *Sierra Nova?*' Michaels asked. 'Or the representatives of the owners?'

Eric hesitated. In a cool tone he said, 'I'm under no compulsion to answer that question. If proceedings go forward in due course, the answer will be obvious, naturally, but at the moment I see no reason why I should explain to you who my clients might be, nor what their interest in the detention matter is.'

'But you wanted to ask Mr Spate questions about the business.'

'I thought he might be able to help me. I did not expect him to be accompanied by someone I do not know.' Eric fixed the man in front of him with a cold glance. 'Just who are you, Mr Michaels?'

A faint smile touched the man's lips; its arrogance did nothing to soften the hardness of the mouth. He reached for the cup on the desk in front of him, tasted the coffee with a notable lack of appreciation, replaced the cup on the desk. 'I suppose there's no reason to keep it secret at this stage. It's quite likely our paths will cross, and even that our interests may coincide. I'm here to co-operate with DCI Spate.'

From the glance Spate shot at Michaels, Eric guessed the cooperation was not welcome to Charlie Spate.

'I'm merely attached to an investigation that is ... ongoing on Tyneside,' Michaels announced smoothly. 'In fact, I work for the IMB – that is, the International Maritime Bureau.'

There was a short silence. Eric was puzzled. He frowned, looked at Charlie Spate, who was hunching in his seat in subdued annoyance. He glanced back to the Australian, waiting.

'Tell me,' Michaels went on, with almost studied casualness, 'have you ever heard of the *Petro Ranger?*'

'I don't think so.'

Michaels unfolded his arms and sighed. 'It's amazing what does, and does not reach the newspapers and the general public. I would have thought you'd have heard about this case. The *Petro Ranger* was a tanker; she was hijacked in April 1998 by twelve Indonesian pirates. She was mastered by an Australian captain and a crew of over twenty men, but they were easily overrun by a gang armed with modern, murderous weapons.'

'Piracy?'

'Precisely. The *Petro Ranger* had sailed from Singapore in early April, headed for Ho Chi Minh City in Vietnam. She should have arrived there two days later. But she never made it. Just nine hours after leaving Singapore the pirates boarded her and from that point on all radio communication with the freighter was lost.'

'That's all a long way from the Tyne.' Eric was puzzled; he glanced at the gloomy features of Charlie Spate. 'I don't understand what—'

Michaels smiled thinly; there was no humour touching his mouth. 'As I confirm, pirates – but don't keep the image of Errol Flynn derring-do in your mind. Pirates have come a long way since the days of the cutlass and the galleon. These days they are more likely to use high speed launches and AK47s, and they've made the South China Seas the most dangerous place in the world for shipping. And they can operate anywhere.' He paused, considering his words. 'But let's stick to the details regarding the *Petro Ranger*. The Indonesian cut-throats boarded her, tied up the crew and the Australian captain, with a *parang* at his throat, was ordered to change course for the Chinese island of Hainan. During the course of this voyage, the name of the ship was painted out, and replaced by *Wilby Adventure*. It had been flying a Malaysian flag; this was replaced by a Honduran one. Once the ship docked at Hainan the cargo was unloaded on to barges. The crew were still shackled below when a Chinese patrol boat boarded, to check the ship's documentation. Everything was declared to be in order.' Michaels was silent for a moment, fixing Eric with a cold glance. 'Why do I tell you about the *Petro Ranger*? Because, I suppose, it illustrates the new level of sophistication reached by pirates in the South China Sea. At the IMB we've been calling this particular case 'the big take'. And it was a big one. You see, the *Petro Ranger* was carrying three million dollars worth of gas, oil and kerosene.'

77

The room was still. Charlie Spate had been listening intently, even though he must have heard the story before. Michaels leaned back in his chair, and continued. 'I could mention other hijackings. There's the *Anya Rose,* still languishing in the mudflats of Beihai; there's the case of the *Tenyu:* she was a Panamanian registered ship which disappeared while carrying aluminium ingots to South Korea. We eventually tracked her down to a port in the Yangtze River. She'd been renamed, repainted, her crew and cargo disappeared. Maybe they were implicated ... maybe they were disposed of by the pirates. We've never found out. But I'm telling you all this to emphasise that we're looking at big business, an internationally organised conspiracy, a hell of a lot of money swilling around into criminal hands, and murder on a considerable scale. That's why I ... and DCI Spate, of course ... would appreciate your co-operation in discussing the ownership of the *Sierra Nova.*'

Eric sat quietly, staring at Chris Michaels, while Charlie Spate remained hunched unhappily beside the tanned Australian. At last, Eric said, 'Are you suggesting that the owners of the *Sierra Nova* are somehow involved in all this?'

Michaels grimaced. 'A few months ago we picked up a man who had taken part in one of these hijackings. He was called Cheung Kiat. We had enough on him personally to persuade him to talk to us and co-operate; the result was we were able to arrest off Johor a ship called the *Pulau Tengah.* We got all the crew, including a real song-bird called Charlie Minh. The pair of them – Kiat and Minh – were able to give us a lot of information – including details of a family of economic migrants that had been murdered in the course of the crew's travels. This is all a very dirty business, Mr Ward. But the point is, the Panamanian ship I told you about – the *Tenyu* – and the *Pulau Tengah* also, if we hadn't managed to find them, they would have been used as cash cows for the syndicate that had employed the pirates in the first instance.'

'Cash cows?' Eric frowned. 'I don't understand.'

Charlie Spate suddenly butted in, as though unwilling to leave the floor entirely to the man from the International Maritime Bureau. 'It seems the IMB has evidence to prove that hijacked ships like these, once they've been repainted, renamed and provided with forged registration documents, they can be put out for charter, again and again. The system would seem to be that unsuspecting shippers, maybe attracted by the cheap freight prices on offer, charter the ships through agencies linked with the pirates and then get their fingers burned. No sooner does the ship leave port with its new cargo than the cargo, the ship and the shipping agent who organised it all disappear into thin air. The reality is that the ship is given a new identity, taken to a different port, and then the scam is repeated. Over and over again.'

Michaels seemed vaguely amused by Charlie Spate's intervention. 'When I tell you that the shipping agent we caught on board the *Pulau Tengah* committed suicide rather than be taken in by us for questioning, you'll realise this business is muscular, big and very serious. In fact, we calculate that this syndicate we're after, they have a hell of a lot to lose. The IMB reckons the phantom ships bring in at least forty million dollars a year.'

'Phantom ships?'

Michaels nodded gravely. 'That's what we call them. Phantoms. If we hadn't found the *Tenyu,* or boarded the *Pulau Tengah,* that's how they'd have ended up. Just phantoms, sailing the seas, disappearing, re-emerging under a different identity.'

Eric hesitated. 'And the *Sierra Nova?*'

Michaels leaned forward, drummed his lean fingers on Eric's desk, frowning slightly. 'The information we got from Cheung Kiat, and Charlie Minh, enabled us to track onto several ships and ports of call. But it's difficult: the phantoms get renamed and repainted so quickly, and so often, that getting hold of them isn't easy. Though it's not the ships themselves we're so interested in, of course, or even the pirate gangs concerned – we want to track down the organisation that operates the system, and bring the major players to justice, close down the business. The *Sierra Nova,* now ... yes, we're pretty certain she's one of the phantoms.'

'*Pretty* certain?' Eric queried.

Michaels gestured vaguely with his right hand. His icy blue eyes were fixed on Eric. 'We've detained the ship. We're checking the documentation. We've found certain irregularities, and are spinning out the whole process. We've been helped, of course, by this smuggling thing about the crew member–'

'Who's been bloody well murdered,' Charlie Spate muttered angrily.

'–but what we are really trying to do is to put some vibrations around,' Michaels went on, ignoring Spate's interruption, 'shake up a few people, introduce uncertainties, so that some of the rats will come out of their holes, start running for new cover. And that's why we'd appreciate your assistance. First, it would be useful to know just who you're working for.'

'And then?' Eric asked quietly.

The blue eyes bored into him. 'Then we'd like to enlist your assistance in further matters. To bring in for us what other information you can.'

'Spy for the IMB, you mean?'

'I wouldn't put it quite like that,' Michaels demurred. There was a note of irritation in the voice.

Eric was silent for a little while. He glanced at Charlie Spate but the policeman was staring moodily out of the window. 'I'm not sure I can help.'

'Why not?' Michaels asked sharply.

'You've told me an interesting tale. Piracy on the high seas. Murder. Fraud. Criminal syndicates. I'm supposed to take all this on trust. Fine, maybe since you work for the IMB, that's what I should do. And since you're clearly on the side of the angels, perhaps I should do even more, as much as I can to help. So, I don't dispute that there are these phantom ships, and maybe the *Sierra Nova* is one of them, but I have a problem in acceding to your request.'

'And just what would that problem be?'

Eric was not deceived by the dangerous softness of Michaels's tone. 'In my business, trust is essential. I am employed, and paid by my clients–'

'We wouldn't expect you to work for peanuts,' Michaels interrupted. 'Your expenses would be

81

covered, and appropriate fees paid–'

'It's not a matter of professional fees,' Eric insisted coldly. 'It's a matter of professional integrity. If I am retained by a client I must respect his interests; if he wants to remain anonymous, I don't disclose his name; anything he tells me, information I obtain on his behalf, that remains with me and him – I don't divulge it elsewhere. And the reason is because I'm merely acting on his behalf, the information is his, not mine, and I can't disclose it without his permission.'

'Legal privilege,' Michaels sneered.

'It's actually *client* privilege,' Eric replied.

Michaels stared at him, his hard mouth twisting slightly. 'I've met shyster lawyers like you all over the world, Ward; you're one of a breed. You cover for criminals; you work with the trash of society; you make life difficult for the good guys – and for what reason? A spurious need to believe in yourselves. To believe in high and mighty principles and expound them, while massive frauds are committed, men die and women are brutally raped and international conspiracies flourish!'

Eric rose suddenly. 'Michaels–' he began.

Charlie Spate was up with him, one warning hand pressed against Eric's chest. 'I think that's enough for now,' he snapped, anger staining his tone. 'Maybe you need time to think about all this. We'll get back to this business some other time. We're leaving now.'

The half empty, cooling cups of coffee and the lingering sensation of vicious anger were all that was left in the room after the two men had gone.

Chapter Six

The car eased its way into the heavy traffic running north on the road past the airport to headquarters at Ponteland. From his seat beside the police driver, Charlie Spate looked back over his shoulder at the silent man in the back of the car. 'Well, you certainly made a pig's ear of that proposal, didn't you?'

Chris Michaels fixed his glance on the stiffness of the driver's back. 'It's guys like Ward who make our job more difficult than it need be.'

'That may be so,' Spate replied sourly,' but you might have handled it a bit more lightly. Ward might have been a copper in the past, and some of the old instincts will still be there, but he's a lawyer now and all lawyers come up with the same bit of crack – they can't disclose client information. But dammit, there's other ways to skin a cat; we got a history, Ward and me, and if you hadn't barged in there with me, maybe I could have got rather more co-operation out of him.'

'I'm used to speaking my mind.'

'Yeah. A well-known Australian virtue,' Charlie Spate scoffed. 'The foot-in-mouth patrol.'

Michaels opened his mouth to respond angrily, but gritted his teeth and thought better of it. The rest of the journey was completed in silence and when they arrived at police headquarters Michaels, clearly still seething with cold anger, got out of the car without a word and marched off in the direction of the administration building. Charlie made his way to his own office, pausing only to snarl at the duty officer that he wanted to see detective sergeant Start in his office as soon as possible.

It was an hour before she put in an appearance. Charlie was still in a bad mood. 'Where the hell have you been?'

Elaine Start raised an interrogative eyebrow. 'Working on the Flinders case. What sand's got under your fore ... fingernails?'

He swore under his breath. But his anger was not really directed at her, or her smart tongue. 'Antipodean bastard,' he muttered. 'I wish I knew what the hell was going on. But the hell with that. And the Flinders case, too.'

'You told me you wanted regular reports,' she reminded him tartly.

'Are you trying to wind me up? You deal with Flinders and, for now, the political flak as well. We got more important things on our plate right at this moment, like the Edwards killing. Have we got an analysis of those bloody tourist tapes from the court yet?'

'We have,' she replied firmly. 'And I've taken a quick look at them.'

'So what conclusions do you draw? Exactly what the hell went on there yesterday?'

'I'll bring both of the tapes in to you later, so you can see for yourself what went down. But briefly, I read it like this...' She paused, waiting, and grudgingly he suggested she might like to sit down. She did so, crossing her legs, but he kept his eyes averted from the distraction of her firm calves. He had to concentrate on matters in hand.

'There are two video cameras that picked up the action. They're not perfect, of course: two Japanese tourists rushing forward to see what was going on, waving their cameras all over the place. One of them is more relevant than the other since it covers Edwards and the people directly related to him. The other camera picks up a different angle, and there's something in there which bothers me. I can't quite make it out, but I'll get back to that later. Anyway, the sequence starts with Edwards being escorted from the courtroom. One tourist was actually zooming in on the courtroom door, thank God. Edwards comes out, flanked by two security officers, with another one out in front. It's at that point, just as he draws level with the camera, that other people come into shot just behind him, and off picture there's a commotion.'

'That'll be the woman shouting the odds,' Spate growled. 'What the hell was she yelling about anyway?'

'Police brutality, what else? But it didn't seem to be related to anything happening on that day. She was just mouthing off.'

'Have we been able to identify her yet?'

'Not yet, I'm afraid. But we're working on it.'

Charlie Spate was silent for a moment. 'I've just been to see Eric Ward. He thinks he knows the face. He was there – saw her when she was thrown out of the building. Find time to have a word with him.'

'I'll do that. Anyway,' she went on, 'it looks as though Edwards must have been looking for a way to make a run for it. Just as some other people – including that barrister who got hurt–'

'Sharon Owen.'

'Just as they come into scene, Edwards looks around, hesitates, sort of jerks and then makes a sudden surge, breaking free and slams right into the Owen woman. She's knocked off her feet, falls against the wall of the witness room and cracks her head. That's almost the first thing you notice: she's directly in focus and the camera picks up her fall. She took quite a blow to the head. She's under observation in the hospital, still.'

'I heard,' Charlie Spate remarked with indifference. He was not particularly interested in Sharon Owen. 'But what about the knifing itself?'

Elaine Start shook her head in doubt. 'It's difficult to make it out. As I say, the tourist was sort of concentrating on Owen at that point. So the rest of it is sort of ... *peripheral.*'

She hesitated, as though expecting some kind of response from him. When he made none, she continued, a hint of disappointment in her tone. 'There's someone just behind Edwards but he's partly obscured by one of the security officers. Edwards makes his dart sideways, collides with Sharon Owen, and seems to stagger almost immediately. It's impossible to see how the blow was struck, but clearly, in the melee, that's when the knife went in. DI Hamilton thinks–'

'Hamilton?' Spate demanded suspiciously. 'What's he got to do with this?'

'He's been viewing the tapes with me,' she said carefully.

'Why?'

'Because he's been assigned to the case.'

There was a short silence, then Charlie Spate exploded into a barrage of obscenities. When he had finished, Elaine Start eyed him coolly. 'Colourful,' she remarked.

He fixed her with a baleful glance. 'Hamilton's been assigned to the case, and no one even bothers to tell me. Just what the hell is going on here?'

She folded her arms. 'I wouldn't know. But I gather you've got plenty on your plate already. This business with the Australian bloke, and the Flinders case...'

She waited while Charlie added to his string of expletives. When he calmed down, she suggested, 'Maybe you ought to take all this up with the Deputy Chief, rather than with me.'

She was right. He nodded, controlled his growing temper. This was nothing to do with Elaine Start. 'All right. Go on.'

'DI Hamilton's pieced it together, he thinks. From the tape he suggests that Edwards was looking for a chance to run as soon as he came out of the courtroom. When the screaming and shouting started, and that woman got ejected, he took a look around, saw that police attention was distracted, and he plunged to his left, knocking Sharon Owen off her feet. But that was his bad mistake; he ran straight into the knife.'

Charlie eyed her curiously. 'This is Hamilton's theory. From your tone, I guess you don't agree with him.'

She lifted her shoulders in a doubtful shrug. 'He may be right – in part at least. But I don't think he was really trying to make a break for it at all. I think he suddenly realised he was in danger.'

'You mean you think he saw the knife?'

'And *then* tried to get away. That's why he was running. But he didn't move fast enough. He took the knife and went down. And then everyone was milling around.'

Charlie Spate was silent for a little while, thinking. 'I'll need to take a look at that tape myself. But I hear what you're saying. What about the killer?'

'Like I said, he was largely obscured. But there's a shot of him, I think, on the other camera angle. Can't be sure. But we'll try to get the lab boys to work on the tapes; see if we can get clearer definitions.'

Charlie leaned back, nodding. 'So, give me the full picture as you – and DI Hamilton, of course – see it.'

'It was a professional hit,' Elaine Start replied calmly. 'No doubt about it. We're both of the opinion that the woman who got thrown out, she started screaming and shouting merely as a distraction, just as Edwards was being brought out. As the security officer on the floor was dealing with her, one of the security officers escorting Edwards was moving away, to help deal with her, and it's only moments after that happens that Edwards turns his head, sees what's about to happen, dives to the left to escape the knife.'

'And doesn't,' Spate mused. 'But how the hell did that knife get in there anyway? They got security on the entrance.'

'There's all hell going on at the court building,' Start replied calmly. 'They're carrying out their own investigation. They think maybe the killer smuggled the knife through security in his shoe, but it's only guesswork. They're reviewing their procedures now.'

'I bet they are. But if it was a professional hit, what could have been the reason for it?'

'As we know, Edwards had been nailed on a drugs charge. Maybe it was something to do with that. His backers wanted him to be kept quiet, perhaps. But I thought you'd be able to come up with a theory, better than me.'

'Why do you think that?' Charlie asked testily.

'Because the man who was killed came off the *Sierra Nova*. And you're the one who seems to be concentrating on that, to the virtual exclusion of everything else.'

'You're back to the Flinders case again,' he glowered, aware of the truth behind her comment.

'You gave me the responsibility for it,' she replied, 'but you also insisted I report regularly. Yet you don't seem to want to know. You spend all your time with your Australian buddy.'

Charlie drummed impatient fingers on his desk. The ache of anger was still in his chest. He wanted to have things out with the Deputy Chief Constable. 'All right. Report now.'

'We've been using all the usual snouts, and we haven't come up with a great deal. But what is clear, there's a deal of nervousness along the river. The three lorries that came in with the cigarettes haul, they're not huge news in themselves, but the word is that they're part of something much more extensive. It's not just that they're simply the latest in a series of runs – we know that from Customs surveillance over the last few months.'

'They should have called us in sooner,' Charlie grumbled.

'The rumours are that it's more than just cigarettes. There's other stuff involved.'

'Drugs, you mean?'

'Not necessarily. Booze, certainly. But, there's some kind of turf war breaking out at the fringe of all this.'

'Bloody hell, that's all we need,' Charlie grunted. 'Gang warfare along the Tyne. I was told those bad old days were long behind us.' He eyed her sourly. 'Anything else that you can't handle?'

'I'm handling this, sir,' she bridled. 'But you wanted a report.'

'All right, all right,' Charlie submitted wearily. 'But you don't think this Edwards killing is linked in, I hope?'

'No link to be seen as yet. But we can't rule it out. And getting back to the Edwards killing, I said there was something on the other tape that was a bit odd, didn't quite gel with me, and I was wondering–'

'All right, yes, fine,' Charlie interrupted. Mention of the killing brought his mind back to her earlier, justifiable jibe. He was playing nursemaid to the man from the IMB, and there was too much else going on to allow it to continue. Flinders, Edwards, they were more important than a fleet of bloody ships that the IMB had carelessly kept losing. He was going to have to have it out with the Deputy Chief Constable, just as Detective Sergeant Start had suggested. 'All right. Get copies of the tapes to me. I'll take a look at them. I've got someone else to see right now.'

Ten minutes later, he discovered that Chris Michaels had beaten him to it.

He stood in front of the Deputy Chief Constable and he knew he was in for a carpeting. He glanced at Chris Michaels, standing a few feet away, risen from the chair where he had been ensconced when Charlie had come into the room. Deputy Chief Constable Dawes had a cold eye and a colder, rasping tongue. He was recently arrived in the north, like Charlie, but there was no question of his regarding themselves as having something in common as new boys on the block. He'd spent his time in the Midlands, and had an unfavourable view about the Met, which had nurtured Charlie. There'd be no favours coming Charlie's way.

'I think you need to be reminded of a few home truths, DCI,' Dawes rumbled menacingly. He was taller than Charlie, bulky, greying and threatening. He had let it be known that he was a hard man who had come up the hard way and was taking no nonsense from anyone in the hierarchy below him.

'Sir–'

'I'm on my feet, DCI, and I'm talking,' Dawes roared. 'First of all, a little protocol. I understand you've been shooting your mouth off in front of a police driver. That's something that never gets done, you hear me? If you got complaints you know where to come. Upwards. You don't sound off in front of a driver, for God's sake.'

Charlie stiffened, shot a glance of pure hatred towards Chris Michaels. 'I thought only Poms whinged–'

'I'm *still* speaking, Spate! Now we've got the bit of protocol out of the way let me get down to the brass tacks of all this. You are under instructions to co-operate with the IMB officer standing here in my office. *Specific instructions*. He's here for a purpose. It's an important piece of business. Your job is to help him, assist him in any way possible, rather than slag him off in front of a police driver, and moreover call into doubt his professional judgment!'

Charlie was beside himself with a rage he could not subdue. 'Professional judgement? Is that what all this is about? What the hell is going on here these days? We got a gang of thugs moving smuggled cigarettes into the area, cigarettes, booze, and God knows what else, and we got the driver of one of their lorries killed in a bloody police pursuit! I'm personally assigned to handle a drugs bust – which turns out to be of little consequence, the amount the man was carrying – and then the guy gets knifed! And what am I supposed to do about all this? First, I'm told to leave the Flinders business to my detective sergeant, *recently* promoted, and now when we got a killing on our patch I'm told to go hold hands with this wallaby here when he's buggering up an interview connected with some bloody ship he calls a phantom. And when I get back from *that* little debacle, I'm told by my detective sergeant – not by you, or the Assistant Chief – that DI Hamilton has been assigned to the Edwards killing without my knowledge! And all you seem to be concerned about is what I happened to say, in my frustration, in front of a bloody police driver!'

Deputy Chief Constable Dawes boasted a very pale skin. Now it seemed almost transparent. His own rage was building up, his eyes glittered like knife-blades and he stood to his full height, shaking slightly, as he glared at his subordinate officer. Charlie suddenly knew that he had allowed his own anger and frustration to take him too far. He waited, shuddering slightly.

'DCI Spate,' Dawes began thunderously, 'I know that you had a certain reputation in the Met, and I am fully well aware that in that force a certain laxity was permitted–'

'Sir.' Chris Michaels had stepped forward, placatingly. 'I ... er ... I think DCI Spate has been a bit overwrought. Maybe that's my fault, after all. But you'll be aware, sir, there are certain issues here...'

Dawes glared at him for a moment and Charlie thought the Deputy Chief was about to turn his rage in the Australian's direction. But then he hesitated, began to cool as he stared at Michaels; something seemed to be passing between them, an understanding, and appreciation, knowledge of which Charlie was unaware. Dawes cleared his throat, turned back to Charlie. 'All right,' he growled, then fell silent. He turned, walked behind his desk, sat down. He put his pale, freckled hands on the desk and his eyes were icy as he looked long and hard at Charlie, slowly bringing his rage under control.

'We're all under a certain strain, here. The fact is ... our cooperation with the International Maritime Bureau is necessary, it's a policy issue, and the Home Office want a senior man involved here as liaison. That means you, DCI Spate. So like it or not, that's what you're going to do. Obey orders. You may feel there's too much on your plate. The Flinders death brings pressure on us and our procedures. I know that the media want an enquiry. And the Edwards business...' His glance flickered briefly towards Chris Michaels. 'The Edwards business will be handled by DI Hamilton. He's already been assigned. But let's be clear. The *Sierra Nova* is high priority. You work with this IMB officer. And you keep within personal boundaries. Is that understood?'

Charlie mumbled assent.

'I didn't hear that, Spate!'

'I understand, sir,' Charlie bit out, his chin up.

Dawes glared at him, wanting to take it further, but decided against it. After a short silence he nodded. 'All right, Spate, you can go.' Then, as Charlie opened the door the Deputy Chief Constable added grudgingly, 'Hamilton's being assigned to the Edwards killing ... it's unfortunate you weren't informed earlier.'

Charlie knew it was the nearest he would get to an apology.

The phone rang just as Eric Ward was leaving his office en route to the hospital. When he realised it was Charlie Spate he felt cold.

'Ward? I'm ringing ... well, to say I think we got off on the wrong foot today.'

'I think we said all we needed to say,' Eric replied.

'Look,' Spate wheedled, 'you got to accept that Strines can get edgy dealing with people from the old country. They've never shrugged off the old colonial mentality: they see all Poms as bastards.

He was out of line, was Michaels. I think you ought to know that's my opinion.'

'It's mine, too,' Eric replied coolly.

'Hey, you're not making this easy for me!' Charlie Spate exclaimed in sudden irritation.

'Should I have to?' Eric asked sarcastically.

'You *owe* me, Ward!'

And he was never going to let him forget it. Eric took a deep breath. Maybe he was being a bit harsh; after all it had been Michaels who had stepped out of line, not Spate. 'Yes, all right, it's something we can regard as over and done with.'

'Good,' Spate grunted. There was a short silence, as he mulled over how to get across what he wanted to say. 'Look, Ward, this *Sierra Nova* business. Chris Michaels pushed too hard, but I'm sure there are ways around all this.'

'I've already explained my position. I can't betray a client's confidences or interests,' Eric replied stiffly.

'I'm not asking you to do that. But, well, you got a reputation along the river. From the old days, and from more recently, since you stepped over the wall, shucked off a uniform and put on a gown. You know people. You got contacts.'

'And?'

'I want... I'd like you to use them. For instance, you said you recognised that woman who was doing all the yelling before she was bundled out. I'd like you to think hard, give us a name we can follow up.'

'And the *Sierra Nova?*'

He could hear Charlie Spate's heavy breathing at the end of the line. 'It's like this, Ward. You

95

don't need to cross your client. You don't need to tell us who he is. But if you could put the word out with a few people ... if you could let us have anything you pick up, that doesn't compromise your client, well maybe we could reciprocate, help things along with your client maybe. Go easy, that sort of thing, when the chips are down.'

'You're not making sense, Mr Spate.'

'Sense enough, I reckon. Do what you can Ward, and no hard feelings, hey? You'll find me at the end of the line.'

He rang off, leaving Eric puzzled and thoughtful. He was still mulling over the implications of the conversation as he drove in the Celica to the hospital at Jesmond.

Sharon Owen was in a private ward, so there was no problem raised about visiting her. She was sitting up in bed when he entered the room. Her hair was tousled, her eyes bright, and she was surrounded with papers on which she had been clearly working. She seemed pleased to see him. He gestured towards the scattered files.

'No bandages. No blood. And the place looks like an office.'

She laughed; Eric was pleased to hear that sound again. 'I feel like a fraud. They insist I stay in for another day, to keep me under observation, but I don't really believe it's necessary. I took a bang on the head, and I've got a tender, large lump on my skull, but I think it's my mixed Irish-Welsh parentage that accounts for its thickness, and consequent resistance to attack. I feel okay. But bored sitting here, with nothing to do. So I rang chambers and got the clerk to bring some file papers in.' She hesitated, glanced at the roses that had been placed on the table beside her bed. 'A nice thought. It's much appreciated.'

He grinned. 'We lawyers have to stick together. You helped me out the other evening; this way I can show my thanks, and reciprocate a little.' He took a seat beside her bed. 'But I still think it's unwise to spend too much time working, in the situation you're in.' He nodded at the files. 'Nothing too heavy, I hope.'

She hesitated, frowning slightly. 'They're relating to the Northern Foods case. You know, the interference with contracts suit being brought against Joe Tilt. Your client and mine.'

Eric laughed. 'Not mine any longer. With the newspaper backing down, he's cleared off my books – or at least, will be when he's paid me.'

'I thought only barristers suffered that way – when solicitors don't pay them.'

'Ouch! Anyway, how's the Northern Foods case working up?'

She shrugged. 'Oh, Teddy Archer is getting a bit edgy about it. Wants the files returned quickly, God knows why, because it'll be weeks before the hearing. He's been pestering the clerk in chambers apparently, says Joe Tilt is putting pressure on him, but clients are always like that. That's why I had the file sent in here. But I've just about worked up the research side, so he can have the damn things back as soon as I'm out of here.'

'Have Northern Foods got a case?' Eric queried.

She scowled at him, mockingly. 'Eric, you know I can't give an opinion without charging you! Well, if what the Manchester company claim is true – or I should say – *capable of proof,* yes, there is a charge to answer. They reckon Tilt has seen strong-arming their established clients, persuading them with some heat, to try to get them to break their agreements with Northern Foods, and tie in with him. But from what I can see, it's all a bit thin. Doubtful testimony, unreliable witnesses, and probably refutable.'

'So Joe Tilt says,' Eric replied, laughing.

'He's never been sent down yet,' she said primly. 'Anyway, to hell with Teddy Archer.'

'You shouldn't ever cross briefing solicitors,' he advised her solemnly.

'In that case,' she retorted, 'if you just let me finish these notes, maybe you can do me a favour and take the files back to my chambers on your way home. Don't you solicitors like sticking together?'

He grinned at her. 'Teddy Archer is a sticky one too far. But, since I still feel I'm in your debt, I'll do as you ask. And when you're up and about again, maybe I'll have the chance to properly repay you for your help the other night.'

'And how, Mr Ward, do you propose to do that?'

'By taking you to dinner.'

Chapter Seven

Eric spent an uneasy twenty-four hours mulling over Charlie Spate's request. He had been annoyed by Chris Michaels, and certainly had no intention of agreeing to his request, but Spate had put him on something of a spot. Spate's request had been pointed, but the problem lay in determining just where the interests of Eric's client might be compromised. Eric still had no idea what was going on with the *Sierra Nova,* and he thought the best way forward was to seek an interview with Paul Sutherland, at Goldwaters, to clarify matters. It was as well to clear the air.

The appointment was quickly made over the telephone, with Sutherland's personal assistant. Clearly, Sutherland thought Eric had information to impart, and was eager to receive it. When Eric was shown into the office at the top of the building, Sutherland was on the telephone. He waved Eric to a seat, while he listened, muttering occasionally in agreement. Eric took the opportunity to inspect his surroundings: expensive, leather-topped desk. Rich, wine-coloured carpet; silver decanter service on the drinks cabinet in the corner; Paul Sutherland would have good reason to get nervous over the fact his board might ask awkward questions. He had a lifestyle to lose.

'Well, Ward, what have you got for me?' Sutherland asked brusquely, replacing the phone. He leaned forward expectantly, clasping his hands together, fixing Eric with a piercing glance in which there was no hint of friendliness. His hard mouth was set; his hawkish eyes hooded carefully.

'As it happens, very little,' Eric replied.

'What's that supposed to mean?' Sutherland demanded.

'It means that I haven't got very far forward, you might say.'

'I paid you a retainer–'

'And I've had a visit from the police.'

There was a short silence, as Sutherland glared at Eric, knitting his brows in an angry frown. After a while, he asked, 'Why would the police visit you? You were engaged because I was assured of your discretion. Have you been careless in making your enquiries?'

'I haven't really had much opportunity to do what you want. And it wasn't just the police who came to see me. There was someone else there too. An inspector from the International Maritime Bureau.'

Sutherland unclasped his hands, leaned back in his black leather chair, and fumbled in the silver cigarette case on his desk. He extracted a filter tip cigarette, flicked open a desk lighter, lit the cigarette and drew on it. He inspected the glowing end carefully as though it held answers for him. Then his eyes narrowed as he looked up at Eric through the curling blue smoke. 'The IMB... You'd better explain.'

'I was hoping that *you* would be able to explain to me,' Eric replied coolly. 'You retained me to discover just why the *Sierra Nova* was being held, suggesting that the reasons given were a bit thin, and you wanted me to dig a bit deeper, see if the drug-smuggling charge against the crew member Edwards played any part in the decision. Since then, the man concerned has been murdered.'

'I saw it on the news,' Sutherland muttered uneasily, smoothing his left hand over his neatly parted dark hair in a nervous gesture. 'I hope you're not telling me–'

'What concerns me is what *you're* not telling

me,' Eric countered. 'Do you know why the IMB are involved with the *Sierra Nova?*'

'I've no idea,' Sutherland replied in a guarded tone.

'They wanted to know whether Goldwaters own the ship.'

'That's none of their business,' Sutherland snapped sharply. 'Or yours, for that matter. But for your information, Goldwaters just arranged the chartering of the *Sierra Nova* for a client. Ownership is none of our concern, although as far as I'm aware she's owned by a company registered in Labuan. But so what?'

'So who has been contracting with you for the *Sierra Nova?*' Eric asked, puzzled.

'What the hell's the reason for this cross-questioning?' Sutherland asked irritably.

'The reason is that I've been asked questions that I can't answer by the police and the IMB,' Eric countered. 'It's left me feeling vulnerable.'

Sutherland drew on his cigarette; some of his earlier uneasiness seemed to have dissipated. 'Vulnerable...' He snorted contemptuously. 'I think we ought to get a few things straight here. I asked you to find out precisely why the *Sierra Nova* was being held, try to determine whether there are reasons other than the ones given. I asked you to find out whether the Edwards issue was one of the reasons why the ship was being held. I did not ask you to start digging into irrelevant issues such as the ownership of the damned ship, or the details of contracts held by Goldwaters! I think you're out of line, Ward, and I'd like to know what the hell you think you're up to!'

Eric was silent for a while. He had a duty towards Goldwater and Sons; he had taken their retainer. It was necessary that he issue a warning to Sutherland, though he was oddly reluctant to do so, because he did not like the man and felt there were matters not being disclosed to him. Nevertheless... 'So you have no idea at all why the IMB are interested in the *Sierra Nova?*'

Sutherland's lean, chiselled features were marked with distaste. 'I've already given you an answer to that. Now, I'm hoping you're going to tell me,' he sneered.

'You've no idea she might be a phantom ship?'

There was a short silence, as Sutherland inspected the end of his cigarette once again. It was a prop, Eric realised, giving him time to think. At last, Sutherland said, 'Phantom ship. What's that supposed to mean?'

'A ship that's been chartered under a name other than its original one; maybe a ship that's been hijacked, renamed, used over and over in scam operations.'

'Is that what the IMB think?'

Eric made no reply. He watched Sutherland carefully, as the man's glance flickered around the room as though seeking answers. At last, Sutherland said, 'I was told you had connections. That you could find out things. That's why you were engaged. All right, you've come up with something. You tell me the IMB are also involved in some way. Do you think their involvement is the reason why the *Sierra Nova* is being held?'

'I've no idea.'

'But they've been to see you. What exactly did

they want?'

'Co-operation,' Eric replied carefully.

Something flickered behind Sutherland's eyes; it could have been alarm; possibly it was calculation. He leaned forward, with a deliberation that was almost menacing. His establishment accent held a sharp edge. 'Co-operation ... that can mean a lot of things. It can mean talking out of turn. It can mean disclosing private and confidential inform-ation. But you're a lawyer. And you've been instructed by me ... and paid by Goldwaters.'

'And that buys my discretion,' Eric commented. 'But if I'm to undertake any enquiries on your behalf, I need to be put entirely in the picture.'

Sutherland stood up, walked across to the window, stared out across the Tyne. He turned, and slowly stubbed out his cigarette in the glass ashtray on his desk. He shook his head in mock regret. 'No. I think we've made a mistake. There is no broad picture I want to paint for you. And now you've been approached by ... other parties, I'm not sure I can trust you any further. I've never held lawyers in high regard, and certainly, lawyers with practices such as yours leave me with more than a little unease. Your original appointment ... it was against my better judgement. So I think we can end our association. I was misinformed about you; I don't think you can help us after all.'

'I'll repay the retainer in the morning,' Eric said stiffly, rising to his feet.

Sutherland held up a hand. His brooding eyes were cold. 'No, I don't want the repayment. When I said we can end our association, I meant I don't want you to do any more research on Goldwaters behalf. But we're still your client, Ward. And that means you don't pass on any information about our dealings to anyone else. We've bought your loyalty, my friend, and your discretion. And if you try returning the cheque, I'll make sure the world knows you're not a lawyer to be trusted. And I do have influential friends.'

Eric nodded slowly, not surprised by Sutherland's reaction or his veiled threat. 'I hear you. And maybe I'll keep your money. I don't feel I've earned it but ... one word of warning. I don't know what you know about the *Sierra Nova,* or its owners, but I would tread very carefully if I were you. Make your own enquiries through other agencies. And naturally, since you are my client, if any interesting information comes my way I'll let you have it. But from what I'm told, this is a very serious business, and the IMB won't give up easily.'

'Give up what?' Sutherland sneered.

'Trying to find out what they want to know.'

As he left the room Eric was aware of Sutherland's glance drilling into his back.

Eric walked back along the Quayside in a thoughtful frame of mind. He had gained nothing from his visit to Goldwaters other than a reaffirmation of his dislike for the man who had retained him; no questions had been answered, but he was certain Sutherland was holding information back from him. He had done his duty, warning the man that the IMB regarded the *Sierra Nova* as a phantom, but he had gained nothing in return. Except a warning off. He was inclined to walk away from the whole business, but he confessed he was intrigued. He stood for a while beside the river, as the gulls whirled and screeched in squabbling disharmony above his head. Then he returned to his office.

When he entered, Eric was surprised to see Detective Sergeant Elaine Start sitting in the waiting room, a cup of coffee in her hand, engaged in deep conversation with his secretary. Susie smiled at him as he came forward. 'I told Miss Start you wouldn't be too long.'

'And the coffee here is better than the rubbish we get at the nick,' Elaine Start commented. 'We've been talking old films.'

'*On Golden Pond* makes us both weep,' Susie informed him.

'And we both loved *My Darling Clementine*. Henry Fonda was a favourite—'

'You wanted to see me?' Eric asked irritably. 'I'm suddenly very popular with the police.'

'All in the line of duty,' Elaine Start said, flicking a glance at Susie, then rising and draining her coffee cup. 'Shall we go in?'

Eric gestured to her to lead the way into his room, and as she walked past he glanced at Susie Cartwright. She pulled a face at him, and then silently mouthed *Nice girl*. Eric followed the police sergeant into the room and closed the door. He shrugged away his momentary irritation. He quite liked Elaine Start. She was straightforward, and had a good sense of humour. 'So, how can I help you?'

'Charlie Spate suggested I talk to you. About what happened at the law courts the other day.'

Eric nodded, frowning. 'The Edwards killing.

I'm afraid I didn't see very much. It was more or less all over by the time I got to the scene. And I was concerned about the young barrister–'

'Sharon Owen.' Elaine nodded. 'Looks like she just got in the way of something unpleasant. But you did see the woman who was doing the screaming, just before Edwards was attacked.'

Eric nodded. He gestured the detective sergeant to a seat and went behind his desk. 'That's right. I heard the shouting, and I saw her being thrown out.'

'Charlie Spate says you think you might have recognised her.'

'It was a long time ago,' Eric replied thoughtfully. 'The face ... the name ... they keep dancing into my mind. But it's difficult to pin down. It's something to do with Shields...'

'When you were a copper?' Elaine Start asked.

'Mmm.' Eric was silent for a while, thinking back. 'I know I've come across her, somewhere. But it's a while ago now. She couldn't have been much more than thirteen, fourteen then. Already on the skids, as I recall. That's right ... the old story. Abused by a stepfather; bit of petty larceny; selling herself to earn a few quid; detention centre where she picked new tricks and a liking for crack ... yes, that's right, I remember now. I pulled her in, material witness to a robbery with violence. Oddly enough she wasn't really involved. Just happened to be there when the off-licence was raided. Young thug with a sawn-off shotgun. The Sikh owner put up a fight, the gun went off, and the thug did a runner. Of course, she seized her own opportunity to grab a few things when the

106

owner went yelling into the street with a gunshot wound. That's how we got her to testify.'

'Threatened to charge her with being an accessory?' Elaine Start queried.

Eric nodded. 'She identified the guy with the shotgun. And received a beating for it, I believe, later.'

'The usual efficient police protection,' Elaine muttered sarcastically. 'Anyway, you clearly remember her. But ... you've got her name?'

'It was a long time ago, like I said ... I'll have to think. It was an Irish name, I recall. Let me think...' He was silent for a while. 'She turned to prostitution, later. On a regular basis. Worked for Mad Jack Tenby when he was running in that business.'

Elaine Start rolled her eyes in despair. 'Oh, God, don't tell me that name. If Charlie Spate hears she used to work for Tenby he'll be crawling all over our reformed gang leader again, to the annoyance of all and sundry.'

Eric smiled. 'I gather Mad Jack Tenby is Mr Spate's *bête noir*. But I don't think Tenby's involved in prostitution these days.'

'So he claims, anyway. We could be convinced otherwise. But this girl...'

'Gullane,' Eric said suddenly, snapping his fingers. 'That's it. She was called Patsy Gullane. I knew there was something familiar about her, when I saw her being ejected ... older now, harder features. But that's who it was.'

Elaine Start nodded in satisfaction, made a note of the name. 'You have any idea where we could find her?'

Eric shook his head. 'No, but if I do come across anything...' He glanced at Elaine, wondering whether she knew anything about the debt he owed Charlie Spate. Her eyes were clear, innocent. But she had worked with Spate on the call girl killing a year ago. 'If I come across anything, I'll be in touch.'

'Appreciated.'

'You think her behaviour was part of a setup?' he asked.

She eyed him shrewdly. 'It's a line we're following up. This Patsy Gullane, maybe she was the diversion, drawing attention away while a knife was slipped in. We need to find her, talk to her ... and if there was no connection, eliminate her from our enquiries.'

'Or find out who she was working for.'

'Something like that,' Elaine nodded. 'The chances are, she was involved. Too much of a coincidence, otherwise, in that kind of sequence of events.'

Eric hesitated. 'Does this killing have any link with the holding of the *Sierra Nova* in any way?'

She looked at him impassively. Her glance gave nothing away, but there was a slight curiosity in her tone. 'Why would you think so?'

Eric shrugged. 'I don't know. But Edwards was a member of the crew. I just wondered...'

Elaine Start sighed. 'I'm just involved in a murder enquiry. Quite why everyone is going bananas over some ship tied up on the river, I don't know. But then, no one tells me anything. Personally, I think it's just a coincidence that Edwards came off the *Sierra Nova,* but there are others who seem ... obsessed with other ideas.' She frowned, perhaps feeling she had said too much. 'Anyway, thanks for your help.'

'Try trawling through some old files,' Eric suggested, rising with her. 'Maybe you'll come across Patsy Gullane's name. What about the man with the knife, himself?'

She shrugged non-committally. 'You didn't get sight of him?' When Eric shook his head, she went on, 'We hope we'll get something off the tourist videotapes, but there's no direct lead at the moment. If we get hold of the Gullane woman, and discover she really was involved, maybe we'll crack it quickly. If not...'

After she had gone, Eric sat behind his desk, thinking. The old days when he had pounded a beat were long gone, but the memories came back now: the dark alleys, the brawls outside the clubs, the occasional river drag, the railway line suicides to clean up, the beatings, the strong-arm clashes... A messy job, a messy life in so many ways. During those years, there had been several gangs along the river, struggling for supremacy. It had been about one-arm bandits, fruit machines, protection money. Things were different now: on the surface quieter maybe, more controlled, but drugs and prostitution were still rife, and there were bigger villainies also, syndicates that were faceless, ruthlessness that was unparalleled. Mad Jack Tenby had been one of the old, crazily violent kind, but he claimed to be reformed now, moving in polite circles. There were smoother operators these days; designer suits, careful accents, legitimate business fronts.

But the rats were still out there, gnawing away at the ligatures of society, under cover of the riverbanks...

He thought back to his conversation with Paul Sutherland. The Goldwaters retainer disturbed him. He felt he was being held on the edge of something; he was unable to understand why he had been brought into the matter in the first place; there were things he was unaware of, reasons and activities that were cloaked by swirling mists of secrecy.

Patsy Gullane. He was glad he had remembered the name. It could help even the score with Charlie Spate. It would certainly achieve that objective if he could find out where she was to be located now. And there was someone who could help him do that. Someone who could help him locate Patsy Gullane – and get Charlie Spate off his back – and maybe find out a little more about the *Sierra Nova* also.

An ex-jockey called Jackie Parton.

Chapter Eight

The lounge bar in the Pig and Pen tended to be fairly quiet in the early evenings during the week. It was an old-fashioned pub: the main public bar boasted a brass foot rail and a wide range of real ales, while the room itself was split up into cubicles by old oak and pine section walls, stained and discoloured by long years of nicotine abuse.

Women were generally not welcomed in the public bar: there was no actual ban upon their presence but if any did come in some of its normal clientele, construction workers and rivermen – or at weekends, football supporters – would glower and mutter that it had been better in the old days, when women knew their place. The lounge bar was different: brighter, more modern, its décor had been a conscious decision upon the part of the licensee to encourage a more up-market trade. He had succeeded to a certain extent: businessmen came in occasionally, with women other than their wives; there was a considerable gay clientele, who seemed to enjoy feeling close – but not too close – to the rougher ambience of the main bar; and at weekends, when the theatre crowd spilled out from Grey Street it could be busy and noisy and exuberant.

Even so, Eric was surprised as he sat in the public bar waiting for Jackie Parton, to see through the hatchway two men he knew standing ordering drinks in the lounge. One of them caught his glance, raised his eyebrows and nodded. He turned to his companion and muttered something; a few minutes later the passageway door opened, and Teddy Archer walked in from the lounge bar, and approached Eric.

'Didn't think the Pig and Pen was your kind of scene,' he said.

'Nor that yours,' Eric replied, nodding towards the hatchway.

'Hah,' Archer grunted dismissively. 'If a client asks you out for a drink after the business is done, needs must go to the pub of his choice. You

111

saw who I'm with didn't you?'

'Joe Tilt.'

'An ex-client of yours, I understand, and an important client of mine. We've been in conference most of the afternoon. Time to relax a while now ... and one must keep in with one's paymasters, hey, Ward?'

'This will be the Northern Foods business,' Eric replied casually. 'How are things going with it?'

'Progressing, progressing.' Archer stood smugly in front of Eric, rocking slightly on his heels. A slight hint of uneasiness crept into his tone. 'Of course, we thought we might have a problem with our barrister being ... incapacitated after that nasty incident at the law courts. You been to see her, I understand?'

'That's right.'

'She's due back at work soon, I'm told.' A leering smile darkened Archer's features. 'So what's your interest in her, then?'

'A friend,' Eric replied brusquely.

'So you're not out to get an inside track from me.' The leer had become more pronounced, but somehow it lacked conviction. 'That's good. I have a feeling I'm getting places with her at last. Beautiful girl. And keen to impress. You know she got Joe Tilt's Northern Foods file sent into the hospital, so she could finish working on it? That's what I call dedication. Or maybe she was out to please me, personally.'

Eric regarded the lawyer calmly. He knew what Sharon Owen thought of Teddy Archer; he was surprised Archer had still not got the message.

'Anyway, nice to see you, but better get back to

my duty.' Archer began to turn then stopped, almost theatrically, as though remembering something of importance. 'By the way, Sharon gave you the file to return to chambers, didn't she?'

'She asked me to do her that favour, yes. Told me you were eager to get the papers back.'

Archer nodded vigorously. 'Yeah, that's right, I picked them up later from her chambers. It's Joe Tilt ... well, you know what he's like. Young man in a hurry. Wants to cut corners. Build his business. Clear away any clutter, like lawsuits. He's been on my back, so I had to chase her up. But I told him, these things take time. So ... what did you think of their case?'

'Whose case?'

'Northern Foods. Personally, I think they'll have trouble making the charges stick against Joe Tilt, but I just wondered–'

'What?'

Teddy Archer injected puzzlement into his tone. He licked his lips nervously, his glance failing to meet Eric's. 'Well, you know, you visited Sharon, and she was working on the file, and I thought maybe you discussed it between you–'

His voice died away uncertainly as Eric stared at him. Eric's tone was cold. 'I asked her what she was working on, because I thought it was unwise of her to do any work while she was recovering in hospital. She was supposed to be resting. So I knew she had the Northern Foods papers, but we didn't discuss the case.'

Archer flapped his hands uncertainly. 'Oh, I didn't mean to suggest... No, I just wondered whether you had discussed it, or whether professional curiosity made you glance at the file when it was in your hands, and I thought that if you did, and had an opinion...' His voice died away to a mumble, edgy, nervous as he noted Eric's expression.

'Professional curiosity can produce dangerous results, that's true,' Eric said. 'But there's the matter of professional ethics, too. It's a strange thing. You're the second person this week who's suggested I'm a bit weak as far as professional ethics are concerned. It's a suggestion that's beginning to be a bit irritating.'

'Ah, now,' Archer insisted hurriedly, raising both hands in nervous protest, 'I wasn't suggesting that you – or even Sharon Owen for that matter – had behaved unethically. I mean, since you had the file for a while, I was just thinking ... and if you had, well, I wondered what opinion you might have formed...'

'I've formed no opinion, Archer,' Eric said coldly. 'I didn't look at the file. I just delivered it to Victoria Chambers. Now, if you don't mind...'

'Of course, of course. Hey look, no offence Eric. I didn't mean–'

'Joe Tilt will be wondering where you've got to,' Eric cut in meaningfully.

'Yeah, that's right, I better move. I ... I'll see you around, Eric.' Teddy Archer backed away, his pale face glistening as he turned back towards the passageway door. It closed softly behind him; Eric saw him through the hatchway, approaching Joe Tilt. Then they moved out of his line of vision. Disgustedly, Eric finished his drink and walked up to the bar. He ordered a large brandy and soda. As the barman brought it forward, he became aware of someone approaching him, standing just behind his left shoulder.

'Villainous company you keep these days, Mr Ward.'

It was Jackie Parton.

The ex-jockey was well known in the Pig and Pen. He merely glanced at the barman and nodded, and the man turned away to pull Jackie a pint of his preference. But then, Eric considered, Jackie Parton was well known in bars all along the river.

Football crowds still roared at Gallowgate and bayed and chanted the names of their recently signed heroes; the football stars of yesteryear were eulogised, remembered, written about and, when they opened bars or clubs, patronised. Jackie Parton was different: the wiry, wizened little ex-jockey was not only remembered – he held the respect of men along the river. He'd been successful as a locally-raised rider at the Newcastle Races and in his day he had earned a considerable amount of money. But in his youth he had been over-generous, and his money drained away. That was why, rumours suggested, he had got involved with the race track gangs; there had been whispers that he had thrown a race – or refused to – and there had been a bad beating as a result. He had retired, but had not faded away: he was still a minor celebrity on Tyneside, and though people were unclear just how he made a living, he was welcomed everywhere, in Shields, Benwell and Byker, Wallsend and Scotswood. While Eric Ward had his own range of acquaintances and contacts from the old days, it was more than matched by

115

Jackie Parton's. The ex-jockey could insert himself into gambling clubs and dives Eric could not; he seemed to know most of the shady characters who moved in the seamy underworld along the river, and he could find out things that Eric never could.

Parton jerked his head sideways to Eric as he accepted the beer from the barman. He led the way to a far corner of the bar, tucked away behind a partition, out of the line of sight from the doorway. Eric sat down on the bench seat beside him. 'Villainous company, you were saying, Jackie.'

'Aye, I was that. Saw you talking to Mr Archer, so I stayed back out of the way.'

'You don't like him.'

'Don't know him well enough to like or dislike,' Parton shrugged. 'But I don't trust him. They reckon he's a slippery customer, the word is that he'd sell wor granny, or his own for that matter, for tuppence. And he runs with a funny crowd.'

'He's a lawyer,' Eric smiled. 'That means he has to keep strange company from time to time.'

Jackie Parton grinned wickedly. 'Like you ... and me, you mean. I get your drift, Mr Ward. But while Mr Archer is regarded as a bit of a shyster, you, well, you always held respect; people knew you were straight.' Or used to think so. Suddenly, the unspoken words were hanging there between them, and Jackie Parton's glance slipped away in momentary embarrassment. He and Eric had had a close working relationship over the years, bordering on friendship, but the ex-jockey had still not entirely come to terms with what he saw as Eric's fall from grace, over the killing of the call girl Sandra Vitali. The thought also reminded

116

him of Eric's personal situation at the moment. 'You seen Mrs Ward recently?'

He had always liked Anne. Eric nodded. 'Things are staying amicable, Jackie. But we're still going ahead with the divorce.'

Jackie's mouth drooped. 'Your business, I don't mean to interfere. But that lawyer she's friendly with, that QC called Sullivan, I get the feeling he's a shyster as well... Anyway,' he went on hurriedly, getting back to more secure ground, 'what I was meaning was that Mr Archer there, he kind of cuts corners for characters he shouldn't even be associating with. As a lawyer, I mean.'

'Such as Joe Tilt?' Eric asked, relieved they'd escaped personal issues. 'I've acted for Tilt myself, just recently.'

'But that didn't put you in his pocket,' Parton retorted.

'Is that how you'd describe Teddy Archer's position?' Eric asked curiously. 'In Tilt's pocket?'

'Who's to say?' Jackie Parton shrugged. 'But I'm told he certainly does a deal of scurrying around for Tilt. And while that may be okay in business terms, it doesn't look good, for a lawyer to be socialising with a man like Tilt in a bar like this.'

'You and I are here,' Eric remarked mildly.

'Agreed, but that's different.' Jackie Parton looked at him levelly. 'My guess is Tilt will be with Archer because he wants to use him and not necessarily on straight legal matters. There's talk that Joe Tilt is getting a bit ... muscular these days. You and me, now, we understand each other. We meet here because it'll be *you* who wants something from *me*.'

'And that's different.'

'In my book.'

Eric laughed. 'Like always.'

'So is it Joe Tilt you want information on?' Parton asked.

Eric shook his head, sipped thoughtfully at his drink. 'No, I've acted for him recently, but I've no interest in Tilt, or Teddy Archer.'

'This guy Edwards, then. The sailor who got knifed. I heard you was there that day in the law courts.'

Eric raised his eyebrows. 'News gets around. Yes, I was there, but saw very little. One thing I did see, however. A woman getting thrown out, screaming abuse. When I'd thought about it a bit, I realised I knew her. Ex-prostitute. Name of Patsy Gullane.'

Jackie Parton's heavy-lidded eyes were hooded. He inspected the contents of his glass carefully, as though it held the secrets of the universe. He drew a slow, deep breath. 'Patsy, hey. Yeah, I was wondering about the scuttlebutt; I'd heard some back lane chat about her and what went down at the courts. You know she's no longer on the game, Mr Ward?'

'Pleased to hear it. But I've heard nothing about her, nor seen her for years. It took me a while to remember who she actually was. She's changed quite a bit, since I came across her last.'

'Haven't we all,' Jackie replied ruefully, rubbing his stubbly, lean jaw with the back of his hand. 'These days, seems she's got what you might call a protector. But what's your interest in her, anyway?'

'I'm under a certain amount of pressure,' Eric said quietly. 'I was able to identify her that time in the law courts, but I've been asked to find out where she is, where she hangs out...'

'Pressure.' Jackie Parton's voice was thoughtful. 'Police?'

'DCI Spate is handling the enquiry into the sailor's death.'

Jackie Parton whistled softly between his teeth. He could not know the story of the relationship between Spate and Eric, nor of the debt that still hung over Eric's head, but he clearly had his own suspicions, unvoiced perhaps, but real enough nevertheless. He tapped his fingers lightly against the side of the beer glass in front of him. 'So they think Patsy was involved in the killing?'

Eric shrugged non-committally. 'They want to talk to her. Want to find out what she was yelling about.'

'You're suggesting it was a diversion. Drawing attention away while the hit was made.' The ex-jockey was silent for a little while. 'I have heard some chatter ... maybe I can make some enquiries ... maybe I can talk to some people who'll be in the know. But, Mr Ward, have you thought much about that killing?'

'Edwards? How do you mean?'

Jackie Parton finished his beer, and rose. 'Well, it was kind of crazy, wasn't it? Think about it, while I get us another drink.'

He made his bow-legged way towards the bar; remained chatting there with the barman for a few minutes before he returned with the fresh drinks. 'What do you mean, crazy?' Eric asked quietly.

Parton shook his head, caressed his stubble in thought. 'Hey, you want to knock someone over,

119

you do it in the law courts? What can be more sensationally crazy than that?'

'Maybe it was the only opportunity available to the killer. Edwards was a crewman off a detained freighter; he was in custody on a cocaine charge. He'd be difficult to get to. But after his court appearance, when he was being escorted out, there'd be a window of opportunity, and with people milling around, confusion–'

'Yeah, I heard there was quite a crowd there that day. Nip tourists, of all things. So ... that what the polis think?' Parton shook his head doubtfully. 'They may be right, I suppose. And there's talk in the clubs... But crazy ... I mean, to do a hit like that calls for a certain kind of nut case, and a certain kind of urgency.'

'How do you mean?'

Jackie Parton half closed his eyes in contemplation. 'Well, the way I see it, to make a hit like that right out in the open, it means some kind of panic is going on. It has to be done quick; there's pressure on to get a result, like *now*. Seize the day. It's kind of unreasoning, you know what I mean?'

'I think so. You believe it has anything to do with the fact he'd been caught smuggling cocaine?'

'Organisation pressure? Trying to ensure he keeps his mouth shut about his dealers? Who knows? Can't say I've heard any whispers of that kind.' Parton paused, squinted around the bar, noting the faces there, keeping a check on shifting groups, movements and acquaintances. 'But the rumours are that this guy Edwards was a bit of a lone warrior, really. I mean, there's no talk of a system, or gang back up, or dealer trouble, you know what I mean?' Parton thought for a little while, scratching his chin. 'Anyway, you say the polis want to know where Patsy's gone to ground. You know I don't much care for working for the fuzz, Mr Ward.'

'Not for the police. For me.'

Parton nodded. 'I'll see what I can find out. And I'll try to get the crack on whether there's anyone we know, like Patsy Gullane, tied in with the killing of the sailor.'

Eric nodded in thanks. He sipped his drink thoughtfully. 'That brings me to the next thing, Jackie. The sailor who was knifed, I told you he came off a ship called the *Sierra Nova*.'

'So?'

'She's tied up; arrested down at Shields. The story is that her documentation isn't in order, but, well, I have a client who wants to find out if there's anything else behind it all.'

Jackie Parton frowned. 'You mean there's a link between the killing and the arrest of the ship?'

'I didn't say that. Maybe there is, maybe not. But there's something odd going on. The International Maritime Bureau are involved. They think the *Sierra Nova* is a phantom.'

'A what?'

Eric explained briefly. The ex-jockey listened intently, eyes fixed on Eric until he had finished. At last he asked, 'Howay, man, this is heavy stuff. So what do you want from me on this?'

Eric shrugged uneasily. 'I'm not sure. Just dig up whatever you can. From the rest of the crew maybe, or people who know them. What's been said around the docks. Like why the ship is really being held ... who the owners are, just what's going on.'

'The docks yes. But checking on the owners, that's different. Not exactly my scene, Mr Ward,' Parton said doubtfully.

'I realise that, but see what you can find out.'

Parton took a long pull at his pint. He wiped his mouth with the back of his hand and peered thoughtfully at Eric. 'You want to tell me what your interest is in the *Sierra Nova*, Mr Ward?'

'Is that important?'

The ex-jockey lifted a narrow shoulder and grimaced. 'Well, it's just that if I start sniffing around in areas where I'm not known too well, I might get asked questions – or I might ask questions of the wrong people. As I said, this isn't strictly my scene. I mean if a freighter is being held, and the IMB are involved in it as well as the polis, it's not exactly small beer, is it? I could start talking to the wrong people; maybe end up in the river myself. If I don't know the score, you understand?'

Eric frowned, considering. He had refused to tell Spate and Michaels who he was working for, but he could see Jackie's point of view. And from long experience he knew he could trust the man's discretion. He nodded. 'All right. I've been retained by a man called Paul Sutherland. He's a director of Goldwater and Sons.'

Jackie Parton bared his teeth, sucked at them. 'Goldwaters? Them with the big office down near the Quayside. I'd have thought they'd have used their own slick fleet of lawyers.'

'Not for this kind of work, it seems.'

122

'Too grubby, hey?' The ex-jockey grinned briefly, then watched him for a little while, uncertainty in his eyes. 'I'm not certain I can help. They're a big company. Not exactly our kind of people. But if it's only finding out some basic kind of inform- ation...'

'Find out what the talk is along the river about the *Sierra Nova*. And if you can discover who owns the ship, that'd be a bonus. As for the Ed- wards thing, well...'

'Now that is my kind of scene. Villainy.' Jackie Parton nodded in agreement. 'All right, Mr Ward, can't promise nothin' but I'll see what I can turn up. Goldwaters, hey... You getting back into the big time, looks like.'

'Hardly that,' Eric disagreed. 'You'll contact me then?'

'As soon as I got anything at all,' Jackie Parton promised.

Chapter Nine

Charlie Spate walked into the incident room. The team were all there already, Elaine Start, DI Hamilton, a small group of detective constables, waiting for him, chatting idly amongst them- selves, empty coffee cups scattered on the tables. 'Right,' he barked, 'let's get up to date. Start?'

'Sir.'

'The Flinders business.'

Elaine Start nodded. 'The media fuss is dying

down somewhat, since we've been able to show fairly convincingly that the patrol car following the lorry with the contraband cigarettes was in fact some distance behind the crash. The lorry driver, Flinders, must have panicked at the junction, collided with the Daihatsu pickup truck, and then turned over on the embankment. I think we've persuaded the local editors that there's no negligence shown, and no evidence of high speed pursuit.'

'Right,' Spate said. 'That's the political flak in hand. What about the investigation generally?'

'We're working with Customs and Excise, of course,' she continued, 'and we've now received Interpol information from Holland, Germany and France. It looks as though we're dealing with a much bigger operation than first envisaged. It's cigarettes, of course, but also booze and various foodstuffs. We think there's going to be another big shipment coming across, in about ten days time, but from what we gather from the German information, there's something else going on as well.'

'Something else?'

'Illegal immigrants.'

'Through Zeebrugge?'

'Into Hull. But ... we can't be certain it's exactly the same operation. It could be that we're dealing with two separate organisations.' Elaine Start hesitated. 'And there's been a shooting war in Stuttgart. I would be suggesting, sir, that we should be putting more time in on all this. I have a feeling that something is going down in Germany which could have repercussions here. If only we'd

124

managed to get our hands on Flinders–'

'Inconsiderate of him to get himself killed,' Spate agreed sardonically. She hesitated. 'And there's something else, sir. The Daihatsu truck, which collided with Flinders's lorry ... as you know, we found no driver in it. And it turns out the truck had been stolen. So...'

'Tell me.'

'So it looks as though one of two things happened. Either some local tearaway had stolen the Daihatsu and when he saw the Flinders lorry bearing down on him he jumped – or maybe was thrown clear in the collision. Or else...'

'Go on,' Spate urged, noting her reluctance.

'Or else the collision was deliberate.'

Charlie Spate stared at Elaine Start in silence for a little while. Someone coughed, cleared his throat and Spate became aware of the growing tension in the room. He guessed she had not raised her suppositions with the other officers, and there was an edge of resentment in the atmosphere. Newly promoted sergeant, trying to make her mark. Defiantly, she raised her chin, held his glance. 'I don't think it's something we should ignore, sir. It's possible that the Daihatsu was waiting for Flinders. It could have been a deliberate ramming.'

'When the police car was on Flinders's tail?' DI Hamilton scoffed, annoyance staining his tone.

'The Daihatsu driver probably didn't know that. We know the police car was some distance behind.' She paused, eyeing Hamilton coldly. 'That's something we've been stressing to the press, to demonstrate we didn't push Flinders

125

into killing himself.'

DI Hamilton opened his mouth to argue, a glint of malice dancing in his eyes. Charlie Spate stepped in quickly. 'All right, all right. Bit far fetched, unless you can get something else to support what you're suggesting. For the moment, just keep your head down on this one, and let us know if anything new develops. Ten days, you say, until there's another consignment? Customs and Excise up to it?'

'We're liaising with them, closely. But I still think sir, that we need more manpower–'

'Forget it,' Charlie Spate interrupted, waving away her suggestion irritably. 'We're talking priorities here.'

'Like the *Sierra Nova?*' she snapped in sudden spasm of defiance.

The silence that followed in the incident room was sharp-edged. Colour slowly ebbed from Elaine Start's cheeks as Spate glared at her; she knew she had gone too far. For a little while Charlie contemplated giving her a verbal roasting there and then, but to some extent he sympathised with her point of view. He decided to ignore the jibe. He shook his head slowly. 'No. Priority ... like a murder.' He looked around him at the silent group. 'And let's look at that now. All ready for the Japanese film show?'

Elaine Start swallowed, then gestured towards the video player. 'It's all set up there, sir.'

Charlie appreciated the hint of humility in her tone. He nodded. 'Then let's get on with it.'

They gathered around silently as the video tape recorder whirred into action. Spate was aware that it had been down in the labs for a few days while the boffins there had worked at it, seeking to enhance the images it contained. They had not been greatly successful, partly because of the quality of the camera work – inevitably shaky and fuzzy in the hands of an excited amateur – and partly because the movement of the main players in the scene was confusing. 'Let's run it right through again,' Spate suggested. 'And then maybe we'll do some freeze shots.'

He watched as the camera of the Japanese tourist began with a brief sequence of the Gateshead Quays, taken through the third floor waiting area window, suddenly pitched and danced as it picked up the bustle of movement near the courtroom door through which Edwards and his escorts emerged. The incident team sat silently as the somewhat blurred figures moved in and out of shot; they could hear the background noise from the woman being ejected, and then there was a slight murmur as Edwards went down, a leaning forward to peer more closely as the confusion and bustling around the stricken man made things difficult to make out. When the sequence was over and the VCR stopped, Charlie Spate leaned back in his chair; he looked around at the tight-faced group. 'All right, Start. You want to begin?'

'I think I should undertake the analysis, guv. Elaine and I have already discussed it at length,' Hamilton chipped in.

Spate regarded DI Hamilton coolly. He knew the type: early promotion, thought too much of his own abilities, quick to take slights, eager to hog the limelight. Maybe thirty now, and hungry for further advancement. Hard-eyed and hard-muscled, arrogant, quick-tempered, mysogynistic. In the old days, Hamilton would have been the kind of copper who would have taken a miscreant down a back alley and given him a good thumping, just to show who was cock of the walk. Now, he'd be more politically correct, with an eye on promotion. But always prepared to jump in, ahead of a mere detective sergeant. Particularly if she was a woman, as well. 'All right, Hamilton, tell us what you reckon you saw on the screen.'

'Perhaps we could run it again, guv...' Hamilton waited as Elaine Start reset the video tape recorder. 'Okay, now here we see, coming along from the left of the screen the first of the private security officers escorting Edwards from the court hearing. If you watch closely, you'll see something seems to catch his attention, just as Edwards and the other two officers appear on the left, just behind him.'

'That'll be when the woman, who we now know was Patsy Gullane, starts shouting and screaming further down the waiting area.' Elaine Start was not to be put off by Hamilton's pulling rank and bulldozing in. And the resentment over dismissal of her comments on Flinders was still simmering. Charlie Spate eyed her for a moment. Good spirit. He looked back at Hamilton: the detective inspector was glowering at her. Then Hamilton turned back to the monitor screen.

'That's right. Patsy Gullane ... she's got a record of prostitution, she's shouting the odds and the first security escort moves out of shot, in the direction of the commotion, to help out the officer dealing with Gullane. If we just freeze the picture there we can see the grouping. The first security escort has moved out of shot, but Edwards and the two remaining escorts are centre. Now just coming in from the right we can see the woman, here–'

'The barrister, Sharon Owen,' Elaine supplied.

'–and then, as we move forward a frame or two, there's someone else just coming into shot at the top right hand edge of the screen.' Hamilton touched his mouth tentatively, and looked around the listening group, pausing for effect before he intoned portentously, 'We think it's the killer we're looking at.'

No one spoke. After a few moments, Hamilton continued, a note of subdued disappointment in his voice. 'Unfortunately, the camera moves at this point, gets blurred as the automatic focus goes haywire and we lose clarity, so that the killer never clearly comes into shot.'

'Although we do have another tourist tape with a different camera angle,' Elaine Start interrupted, 'where it's possible to see–'

'And then, in the next frame we see Edwards beginning to make his move,' Hamilton cut across her as though she had never spoken. 'His head turns, he glances left ... probably realising he can take advantage of the disturbance down the hall, with one of his escorts being distracted, and he takes a dive sideways. Here we can see how he cannons into the Owen woman, and she is knocked against the wall. There's a sudden surge from the escorts, the man at the top of the screen has now come forward and is partly

129

obscured by Edwards, and it's just at this point that we think the knife goes in. The barrister is slumping against the wall, Edwards is going down, the escorts are closing in on Edwards, and the killer – because we think it really is him – is now moving away, head turned so we can see only the back of his head, and is out of shot.'

Charlie Spate held up his hand, to stop the tape. 'The escorts ... they didn't see the knifing or the killer?'

Hamilton hesitated, then shook his head. 'We've interviewed them at length. Taken them through a viewing of the videotapes as well. Fact is, they saw that Edwards was trying to do a runner and they were concentrating on him. They grabbed for him as soon as he lunged forward, but they weren't paying all that much attention to the other people around. And once Edwards was down all hell seemed to break loose; they were leaning over him, kneeling beside him, the Owen woman was against the wall, concussed, and there was just one hell of a flap going on, with the Jap tourists running in all directions, some trying to get away, others clicking their cameras and focussing their video cameras. It was maybe half a minute before the escorts got their heads cleared, understood that Edwards had been hit. That's when one of them gets the blood on his shirt. Time enough for the knifeman to walk away, detach himself from the group, get the hell out of there. And just walk out of the building on the ground floor.'

'Bloody idiots,' Spate muttered. 'That's what comes of using private security services. Why the hell weren't we using our own people, anyway?'

There was a short silence. Then Elaine Start glanced in his direction. 'We thought maybe you would know the answer to that one, sir.'

Charlie Spate glared at her, not understanding. 'Why me?'

She shrugged. 'It seems the directive came from the top.'

A worm of doubt and suspicion wriggled in Charlie Spate's brain. He frowned, chewing at his lower lip. Something was going wrong here, badly wrong. Something he had to sort out. Later. 'All right, that's how DI Hamilton sees it. Any other interpretations coming forward?'

There was a brief murmuring, a few heads being shaken. Charlie was aware of Elaine Start's hesitation: she was wary of stepping out of line again. He looked at her, raised an eyebrow. 'You want to add something?'

'Well,' she said with a degree of reluctance, 'I am in line with most of what DI Hamilton has put forward, but if we take a look at the other videotape...'

They waited in silence as she removed one tape and inserted another. As she leaned forward over the machine, the line of her skirt tightened against her thighs and Charlie Spate watched appreciatively. He liked a woman with spirit ... and Elaine Start had a good body too. Well-proportioned, fine breasts ... he'd have to do something about the way she affected him. One of these days. She turned, caught him watching her, read something in his glance. She raised a cool, mocking eyebrow. Charlie looked away, folded his arms, turned to glance at DI Hamilton out of the corner of his eye. The man was not pleased with Detective Sergeant Start, but Charlie had no problem with that. Let the cocky bastard be taken down a step or two. He was on Elaine's side on this.

'As you'll see,' Elaine Start began, 'this particular camera angle, from the second Japanese tourist camera, isn't as useful or relevant as the one DI Hamilton's been using. And in a sense, it's more confusing, because it almost redefines the relationships between the people in the earlier shots.'

'So why are we looking at it then?' Hamilton asked nastily. 'It doesn't give us a better view of the killer.'

'No, but I think it raises some doubts on part of the suggestions you've made.'

Charlie Spate leaned forward, inspecting the screen. 'Such as?'

'Well, sir, I don't think Edwards was trying to do a runner. You see? He's coming along with his escorts; the first escort walks away out of shot towards the Patsy Gullane disturbance, and here … look … Edwards is turning his head.'

'Looking for his escape route,' Hamilton muttered.

'I'm not so sure,' Elaine Start replied doubtfully. 'To me, it seems he's seen something … or maybe recognised someone.'

'His killer, you mean?' Charlie Spate asked slowly.

'It's possible. Maybe he actually knew the killer – who still can't be identified even on this sequence – recognised him, or maybe he just saw the knife. And that's when he breaks, runs for it, cannons into Sharon Owen – almost deliberately, seems to me – but isn't quick enough. Somehow in this whirling scrum as the escorts grab for him, the knife goes in, he falls, and the killer walks away in the ensuing panic.'

'Just like that,' Spate muttered.

'I think all this is simply a matter of detail,' DI Hamilton grumbled, unconvinced. 'What difference does it make whether Edwards was breaking away because he saw his killer, or because he wanted to do a runner? It still comes down to the same thing.'

'But if he saw the killer, and knew him – rather than just seeing the knife, or making a run for it – we should be considering the possibility that maybe he was another crew member, in which case it's possible other members of the crew can help us identify the man who killed Edwards.'

'We've had no luck so far,' one of the incident team muttered at the back of the group. 'All the statements we been taking, none of them even reckon they knew Edwards very well. Joined the *Sierra Nova* when they docked at Amsterdam, and kept pretty much to himself. And they all naturally deny they knew anything about his drug smuggling activity.'

'But there's another thought that occurs to me,' Elaine Start began. 'What if–'

Charlie Spate held up his hand, interrupting her. 'No more theories at the moment, for God's sake. We got to get the legwork done. Start, you stay with the Flinders business. See if you can come up with something more positive than what you've given us so far. Find out what you can about that Daihatsu. And, all right, follow up the thought that it might have been a deliberate ramming of the lorry we were following. As for Edwards, this is Hamilton's show, here. That's official.'

Elaine Start did not like what she heard, and it showed in the set of her mouth. Doggedly ignoring her displeasure, Spate continued, 'So the first priority is to get hold of Patsy Gullane. It's possible she'll be the key to all this. So try all her known haunts, going way back. Check on her acquaintances, pimps, club bouncers, hotel clerks who might have been slipped money to accommodate her trawling for sex, leave nothing to chance, no stones unturned. Me...' He caught Elaine Start's cool glance. 'I got to go have a word with the Deputy Chief Constable. Again.'

In the event, he did not have to make an appointment. The call was out for him. And when he got to the office it was now no surprise to see that Chris Michaels, once more, was there ahead of him.

'You wanted to see me, sir?' Spate said to the Deputy Chief Constable, unable to hide the edge of irritation in his voice.

DCC Dawes glanced briefly at Michaels, then nodded. 'Take a seat, gentlemen. I gather, DCI Spate, that you've been holding a briefing in the incident room.'

'That's correct, sir, and I–'

'You cover the Edwards enquiry?'

'Of course. And I was wanting to see you about that, sir.' Charlie felt a tingling of anger in his veins. 'It seems to me that someone else is pulling all the strings in this business, and I don't feel I'm being properly informed. To start with, when this crewman was arrested off the *Sierra Nova*, I understand it was the result of a tip-off.'

'That's right. Customs and Excise,' the Deputy Chief Constable admitted, glancing at Chris Michaels. 'We were called in at that point, when the ship docked.'

'The record shows that Edwards was then charged with cocaine possession, and clapped up in the nick. But when he went to court, how come we didn't find an escort from among our own people?'

Dawes hesitated. 'As you are already aware, Spate, we have manpower problems. And it's not unknown for us to use outside security services.'

'Not in cases like this,' Charlie insisted heatedly.

'The decision was taken. We don't need to go into details here.'

'But the result was that the incompetent bastards who were supposed to be escorting Edwards managed to get him killed! Moreover, we don't seem to have put any pressure on these guys, or their employers, to explain exactly what went on, and why they let all this happen! I don't even know which firm employed those idiots. But I imagine you do. Sir.'

Dawes picked up a pencil from his desk, fidgeted uneasily, rolling the pencil between his fingers. 'I've told you. Decisions were made. That's all you need to hear. Now, as far as the investigation is concerned, what steps are you taking?'

Frustrated, Charlie bit out, 'We're trying to trace the woman who created the disturbance. Once we get hold of her, maybe we'll have a handle on who killed Edwards. Meanwhile, I want another crack

135

at the crew of the *Sierra Nova* – since I am supposed to be working with Mr Michaels here on matters relating to the freighter – and then...'

Dawes raised his hand imperiously, silencing Charlie. 'I think I've already made it clear you're to step back from this enquiry. In fact ... don't devote too much manpower to it.'

'This is a murder enquiry, sir!' Charlie flashed. 'I can't believe you don't want high priority given to our finding out who killed Edwards, and why the killing was–'

'We already know who killed Edwards,' Chris Michaels interrupted coldly. 'And why.'

There was a long, icy silence in the room. Charlie Spate stared at Michaels in exasperated frustration. 'What the hell are you talking about?'

The Australian turned his close-cropped head towards Dawes. 'I think, sir, we'd better fill Mr Spate in on all the details.'

'I understood this was a need-to-know situation,' Dawes warned.

Michaels smiled thinly. 'I believe DCI Spate feels he does need to know.'

'Too bloody right,' Spate snarled.

'It's necessary,' Michaels said quietly, 'that the scope of the investigation into Edwards's death is ... contained, and urgencies cooled down. Your first question concerned the security escorts. You want pressure put on them, and on their employers. It's not necessary.'

'Why the hell not?'

'Because we already have all we need from them.'

'How do you know that? Our interviews were

136

like talking to brick walls! They claimed they knew bugger all!'

'They'd already made their reports,' Michaels replied grimly. 'To me.'

The atmosphere was frosty. Puzzled, Spate glanced at the Deputy Chief Constable, and then back to Michaels. 'I don't understand.'

'The escorts weren't employed by an outside security firm. They were part of my own team.'

'They were IMB men?'

'Exactly.'

Charlie Spate glared at him. He was aware of a slow churning in his gut. 'What the hell is going on here? Why would you use your own men to escort a drug-smuggling sailor to and from court? You think we couldn't do a proper job? You put bloody amateurs on it instead—'

'They weren't there just as escorts,' Michaels interrupted. 'They were there to protect Edwards.'

'And a bloody mess they made of that too, didn't they!' Charlie Spate stopped, suspicion sliding into his mind. 'To protect him? You mean you were *expecting* an attempt on his life? But I thought he was small fry, unimportant—'

'We weren't *expecting* an attack, as such,' Michaels snapped in sudden anger. 'It was just a precautionary measure.'

'I don't understand this,' Charlie muttered, shaking his head. 'Why would you want to protect this guy, by putting IMB officers in to escort him?'

Chris Michaels hesitated, glancing at the Deputy Chief Constable. 'Because ... because Sammy Edwards was one of our own.'

'What? Are you telling me—'

'Edwards was an IMB officer. He had been planted on the *Sierra Nova*. He was acting as our eyes and ears. He was pulled off for debriefing when the freighter was arrested, and to make ... certain people less suspicious, we got him charged with cocaine smuggling, locked up safely. There was no drug offence, of course. But we had to go through the court procedures, to keep the story going. There was always the chance that his cover would be blown, and we thought it safer to ... well, it didn't work out. We didn't expect a killing, we didn't think the people we're after would have been so nakedly stupid as to go for Edwards. But they did. And he's gone. All we can do now, is go for these people, pin them down. Get a result. But it won't help if you have your people sniffing along tracks that might warn off the men behind this whole business. We don't need a thorough investigation into the killing, because we know who's behind it. And we're close to getting our hands on the bastards!'

There was a brief silence as both men stared at Charlie Spate. Then Charlie Spate exploded.

Chapter Ten

The network was very much like a spider's web. It was as though Jackie Parton touched part of the outer edge of the web and it shivered, sending slight, covert messages along all the individual strands, reaching dark places, alleyways of information, whispered recesses where people made suppositions, raised possible links, suggested names and activities, arranged for hidden spiders to come scuttling out of dusty corners for favours, or money, or friendship.

There were bouncers from the night clubs, who saw a great deal and heard more; a few underpaid cashiers in bookmakers' offices; there were croupiers in gambling houses who were dangerously on the fiddle, and there were rivermen and long haul lorry drivers, corner shop owners and cabbies, and racing men who frequented a pub in Byker called the Horse and Jockey. It was a different, harder clientele at The Hydraulic Engine on the hill above the river at Scotswood, and a different atmosphere at the Irish Free Hall in Benwell where Jackie was always greeted with free drinks from the inveterate gamblers who inhabited its dusty, dilapidated, Guinness-odoured corners. Down near the docks at Shields, he could have private conversations on the darkly-glistening cobbled streets, pick up rumours and gossip off the freighters, and glean well-ripened snippets from old men who had seen it all before and could put things into an older context – but the sum total, as Jackie was well aware, could be a tumbled confusion of information. He was never direct in his questioning, usually casual, listening more than speaking, putting in an occasional prompt. He found it odd sometimes, the way men who were living on the edge, where violence lurked in the shadows, where loose talk could be dangerous, or where a wrong word could end with a knife between someone's ribs, odd that people were prepared to talk. For some it was because they were loose-mouthed; for others, it was because it brought a feeling of involvement, importance into their lives. With some it was money exchanging hands, or a few drinks poured down receptive throats.

But none of them were ambitious men or women. The prostitutes who talked to him did so because they liked him. The sporting men still held admiration for his recklessness in the old, racing days. The majority talked because they liked talking, it made them feel important, part of the rich riverside scene, aware of community, untouched by the grand new roads and the splendid tall buildings that had changed much of the face of the old Tyneside. And they all were prepared to talk, or gossip, or offer surmises because they knew their names were safe with him, whatever use he might make of the information they supplied.

But it was the barmen who were able to help most. They spent their lives in a frantic, rushed serving of the mass of men and women who poured into the pubs in the evenings, or a casual, relieved leaning against the bar polishing a glass in the slack times. The pub conversations washed over them; an odd word or phrase would catch their attention; drunken confidences would be exchanged, even more drunken confessions imparted in the small dark hours when loneliness demanded a hearing. On Saturday nights after the match at Gallowgate, when the occasional bottle was smashed and things got ugly, once the fighting was over and the police had taken statements and departed, whispered discussions of the reality behind the mayhem would be delivered. A woman, a deal, a contract, a broken promise, or an underworld vendetta. No single barman could ever give a full story, Jackie had learned, but by talking to several, in different pubs along the river, it was possible to build a picture, sketch and paint a wide canvas where the details remained blurred, but the general view would emerge.

And once the canvas was stretched before his mind and imagination, Jackie Parton had the innate ability – sharpened by long experience drawn from the back streets and quiet dockland corners of the Tyne – to sketch in some of the details, fit jigsaw pieces together until they made sense, dredge facts out of a distant past and knit the whole together to create a patchwork for the present.

It was that ability that eventually drew him to the reach of the river beyond Corbridge. He had been able to discover an address, a name, a location. But he was too late. When he arrived at Corbridge and crossed the river, it was only to learn that the police had already found the woman Jackie was attempting to speak to. But she was no longer able to speak to anyone.

The Romans under Agricola had spanned the river at Chollerford a millennium ago as they entered the tribal territory that extended northwards as far as the Firth of Forth. The wild Celtic hordes had been pushed back and the bridge had been built to link the forts and bases on Hadrian's Wall, the supply route running through Corbridge and Chesterholm, along the Stanegate. The re-

141

maining stone supports of the ancient Roman crossing were still to be seen at Chesters Fort, but the bridge Eric now traversed was mediaeval in construction, narrow, solid, arching with stolid grace across the rushing waters below. He drove across, negotiated the roundabout and pulled into the car park of the George Hotel. He sat there in the car for a little while, thinking back to when he and Anne had come here, years ago, then he shrugged aside the memories, got out, locked the car and walked into the gardens of the hotel.

The late afternoon sun glinted on the rippling, bubbling waters beyond the bridge. The manicured hotel lawns sloped greenly down to the riverbank and he caught a glimpse of a heron, flapping its ungainly way from the shallows, something silver glinting and wriggling in its beak. The long legs of the predator trailed behind as it rose and circled towards the far bank, wide wings beating slowly. Eric glanced at his watch; Jackie Parton had suggested they meet in the hotel bar at four-thirty, since business had brought Eric to Corbridge. Eric was a little early, so he sat on a bench and for a while enjoyed the sunshine, the chuckling sound of the river, and the occasional dipping flight of wagtails, the excited flurry of squabbling ducks at the water's edge.

When he heard another car pull into the car park he rose and walked towards the stone-arched gateway. Jackie Parton, in windcheater and jeans, was getting out of his car. He grinned at Eric. 'Not often I get out this part of the world,' he said. 'Used to be racing at Hexham often enough in the old days, so it brings back memories, but I don't seem to get the opportunity to come out here much now.'

'So you grabbed at the chance since I was in Corbridge?'

Jackie Parton squinted into the sunshine, looking about him appreciatively, and shook his head. 'Not exactly. As it happened, it was convenient. But I'll tell you. We got things to talk about. Shall we go inside?'

Jackie led the way into the hotel, nodded to the girl at reception and turned right, down the corridor to the bar that adjoined the dining room. After a few minutes the white-jacketed barman emerged from the side entrance. 'Gentlemen?'

'Quiet afternoon,' Jackie opined. 'Been hit badly by the foot and mouth outbreak?'

'Gets busier later,' the portly man replied, unwilling to discuss the downturn in business.' 'What would you like to drink?'

Eric moved forward to order the drinks while Jackie walked across towards the window. The white-clothed table he chose looked out over the gardens. 'Used to come out here years ago, just for special occasions,' he said as Eric joined him with the drinks. 'Not really my scene, though. Bit upmarket. Still...' He raised his glass in silent salute to Eric, and sipped at the dark liquid. 'Business sorted at Corbridge?'

Eric nodded. 'Property dispute. Farming family. It won't get to court. I persuaded the would-be litigants that if they didn't reach an agreement, what remains of the estate could be drained away by litigation costs.'

'Doing yourself out of work, then?'

'That's part of the job,' Eric grimaced. 'Anyway, meeting here at Chollerford, is it just a matter of getting away from Newcastle for a day out?'

Jackie Parton shook his head slowly, his eyes clouding somewhat. 'No, not really. I been up to Wark again, making a few more enquiries. You know Border Mires?'

Eric considered for a moment, thinking back, then nodded. He had been there occasionally with Anne, in the early days of their settling at Sedleigh Hall, when there was so much of the Northumberland fells and forests for them to explore together. Remotely situated in Wark Forest, a little way west of Stonehaugh, Border Mires consisted of a fragmentary mire system of relict peat bogs and fens. Largely unspectacular and dull, it was yet capable of displaying un-suspected richness of colour on occasions, with extensive carpets of sphagnum moss and rare bog plants. 'Biologist's paradise,' he suggested.

Jackie Parton drew a slow breath. 'That's how it came about,' he said quietly. 'Some guy, amateur biologist, he was up there at the weekend, came over Haining Head Moss, looking in the wet area there. Collecting it seems, cranberry, bog asphodel and sundew.'

Eric was amused. 'Didn't know you were into that sort of thing, Jackie.'

'I'm not,' the ex-jockey replied shortly. 'But it's what the polis got told.'

'Police? How do you mean?'

'This biologist found more than he was expect-ing. He came across the body of a woman in the peat bog. Scared the hell out of him. Scarpered back to Wark as fast as his legs would carry him; polis got called. They was crawling over the place within a couple of hours, just before I arrived in the area, to follow up the leads I'd been given.'

Eric stared at him, a cold feeling touching his spine. 'Your leads,' he repeated dully.

'The woman you asked me to check out. Patsy Gullane. I'd been given an address, a safe house she might've been using. But ... too late. That's who was up there at Border Mires. Patsy. Head bashed in, it seems. So if you was hoping to find out what exactly she was up to at the law courts that day, well, you're not going to hear it from her.'

Eric was silent for a while. At last, he asked, 'Better fill me in.'

Parton shrugged. 'Not a great deal to tell, really. I been asking around all week, and finally managed to find out that Patsy was living with a guy called Billy Leven. Don't know if you ever came across him. You remember the Liverpool gun wars, few years back?'

Eric frowned thoughtfully. 'Vaguely.'

'There was a lot of fuss about it at the time,' Jackie Parton explained. 'Liverpool's got its own reputation: docks like Newcastle, river rats, gang wars, fighting over drug-dealing patches, Catholics and Proddies, you know how it goes. But about five years ago it really got out of hand. A lot of the young villains, they decided fists, crowbars and broken bottles wasn't sophisticated enough. Or as final. They took to using shooters. The local polis took it seriously; they moved in hard and really went to town on the local gangs. Took them two years to sort it, but they got a lot

145

of the lads inside. Those they didn't, drifted – Manchester, Leeds, London.'

'And Newcastle?' Eric asked.

'Billy Leven,' Jackie said, nodding. 'Big lad, reddish hair, bit of a muscleman when he was a kid. Tried Mr Universe, but got nowhere nearer than quarter finals locally. And the rumour is he only got that far by privately beating the hell out of two of his rivals. With a tyre iron.'

'Nice character,' Eric observed ruefully.

'But committed, you might say. Focused. Anyway,' Jackie went on, 'Billy Leven moved to Tyneside when things got too hot for him in Liverpool, soon found a niche for himself. Worked with Mad Jack Tenby for a while, but he was a bit too wild for Jack – you know, Mr Tenby wants the hint of muscle for what he's got going these days, not the actual bruises and broken bones themselves. Last I heard, Billy Leven seems to have been working for one of your clients.'

Eric raised his eyebrows in surprise. 'Who, for God's sake?'

'Joe Tilt,' the ex-jockey advised. 'It's all a bit unclear in what capacity he was on Joe's payroll, but I think it's just protective muscle. The story is, there's a bit of a rumble going on along the river at the moment. That story that got printed in the newspaper about Joe Tilt–'

'That I was to deal with, to get a withdrawal of the allegations?'

'That's right. Well, it seems there was more than a bit of truth in it all. Okay, maybe the journalist just didn't have the evidence to back up the story–'

'That's how it appeared to me, when I challenged them,' Eric suggested.

'And it may be so. On the other hand, maybe their ... retraction was brought about not just by your legal threats. Could be there was a bit of muscle involved as well, or at least, the threat of it.'

Eric was silent for a little while, sipping at his drink, watching the sunlight glittering on the river, a lone fisherman patient on the far bank. At last, he sighed. 'Well, it's over now. The newspaper retracted; paid a cheque to a charity. There'll be no litigation. But what has this all got to do with Patsy Gullane?'

'Oh, hell, I don't know,' Jackie retorted, with a hint of irritation. 'Nothing, probably. There's only so much you can get to find out, you know what I mean? And it tends to be like a scattered pile of old bones: you got to pick through it all to find the specific bits you want to put the skeleton together. It's just that when I heard that Billy Leven was working for Joe Tilt, it seemed to me it was something you ought to know. And it all seems to be part of a bigger turf war in the north-east. Joe Tilt has ambitions, and he's been pushing hard to get bigger control of the food distribution business and he's been meeting resistance. There's talk that it's a struggle with established connections, who work from a base in Manchester, but it's all a bit vague at the moment. Rumours, not facts. Anyway, it's not really anything to do with what you asked me to find out. I just thought you needed warning. Joe Tilt could be trouble.'

'I hear you. But Patsy Gullane?'

'Yeah,' Jackie Parton sighed. 'She got out of the

147

game about a year ago. Shacked up with Billy Leven. And that fracas at the law courts – no one seems to know what it was all about. She was yelling about infringement of human rights, it seems. Imagine! Patsy Gullane! Then she got ejected, and since then, no one seems to have laid eyes on her. But, eventually, a couple of whispers came my way. I don't need to tell you my sources, of course–'

'Don't want to know them,' Eric replied.

'Well, couple of people suggested that there was a safe house up in Wark. Me, I'd have said that the place was too small for someone to get her head down, and maybe she wasn't doing that anyway, just taking a holiday from Billy, who knows? So, I thought I'd check it out, sniff around a bit before I called you. But I was too late. Time I got to Wark, she was found up at Border Mires.'

'Any theories sculling around?' Eric asked.

'Who knows at this stage? Maybe Billy Leven's involved, but there'd been no talk of a bust up between them. And he seems to have gone AWOL anyway. Maybe she couldn't stay away from the game. The local buzz is that maybe she found a punter who got violent, bashed her head in when he couldn't perform, hell, you know it happens. Then dumped her up at Border Mires. Fact is, Mr Ward, I didn't count on crossing this kind of track. You asked me to find out where she'd got to; I didn't expect to learn she'd snuffed it. And by now, I've no doubt your friend Charlie Spate will know all about it.'

'No friend of mine,' Eric replied feelingly.

Parton finished his drink, raised his eyebrows

and Eric shook his head. He had the drive back to the flat at Gosforth, and a faint prickling at the back of his eyes warned him that another drink could cause problems for him. When Jackie returned with a pint for himself, Eric said, 'In view of what you tell me, I guess there's no need for me to talk to Spate about the business at all.'

'It's your call,' the ex-jockey replied. 'Though it would be appreciated if you didn't need to talk to Spate. I don't like giving you stuff for the polis. I got my reputation to uphold along the river.' He paused, wrinkling his seamed brow. 'But, talking of DCI Spate and the polis, it's kind of odd, there's something else funny going on, the way I see it. That Edwards killing, there's been no sort of pressure along the river, you know what I mean? It's as though the polis aren't all that interested. And even with Patsy Gullane ... I know it's early days, but the impression's going the rounds that the fuzz are not exactly getting their knickers in a twist about it. They seem to be buying the crazed sexual maniac line. Just not pushing their usual sources, know what I mean? So, maybe you're right. Stay out of it. Let the boys in blue get on.' He hesitated, eyed his drink for a little while. 'Then there's the other business you asked me about.'

Eric noted the reluctance in his tone. 'The *Sierra Nova?*'

Parton inclined his head. 'You told me it was Goldwaters who had a deal with you.'

'I was retained by one of their directors. Guy called Paul Sutherland.'

'Ahuh.' He squinted at Eric inquisitively. 'You know he went to Sedbergh School?'

149

'Is the fact important?' Eric asked, puzzled.

Jackie Parton sighed. 'You know, you meet all sorts down along the river. Solicitors, ex-army captains drummed out of the forces, alcoholic doctors, and sometimes, people like Posh Harry. I think you might recall him, from years back.'

Eric considered, thinking. At last he nodded. Harry le Frenais, he called himself, but Eric always felt it could not have been his real name. And Tynesiders who knew him well called him Posh Harry. An interesting man: tall, immaculately suited, languid of manner, mid-forties now. A con man, with a persuasive manner, whose personal inclinations had been the running of insurance scams because he had the accent for it. His activities had given him a broken nose a couple of times, when he'd dealt with the wrong people. He wore the scars to his face and his reputation with an air of pride, as though he had in some way proved himself to the world.

'Not seen too much of him in recent years,' Parton continued reflectively. 'I reckon times have been bad for him: people have got wise to his scams. You know, his suit looked a bit shiny, bit of fraying to the collar, that sort of thing. But unlike most of the characters I meet up with, he's got a sort of computer in his head for tying in all the dodgy upper-class people who might be up to something in the city. Me friends, now they are mainly low-life. Posh Harry ain't my friend, but I know him, and for a couple of malt whiskies – well, more than just a couple, more like a bloody bottle – he gave me the low down on the little list he keeps in his head. Believe me, it's incredibly detailed. So, Paul Sutherland, it seems, went to Sedbergh School and then Cambridge. Read Modern Greats, whatever the hell that means. Did a stint in the City of London, whizz kid who got his fingers burned in the Stock Exchange crash, moved north into Goldwaters, and shipping insurance.'

'And insured the *Sierra Nova?*'

'It would seem so.' Jackie Parton was hesitant, choosing his words with surprising care. 'Posh Harry was quite talkative about Paul Sutherland. Hinted they'd tried a scam together at one time, before they fell out over something or other and Sutherland gave Harry the old heave-ho. The experience left a bruise on Harry's ego. He don't like Paul Sutherland.'

'He has that going for him, at least,' Eric murmured.

Parton shot a quick look at Eric; when he returned the glance Parton lowered his eyes, fiddled with the rim of his glass, tracing his finger along its lip. 'Talking with Posh Harry gave me some information. Can't say he was able to tell me who the owners of the *Sierra Nova* might be,' he said slowly. 'But I persuaded him to talk to a few of his acquaintances – for a price – and he finally got back to me with something. I can now tell you that the ship was the subject of a charter deal arranged through a Singapore company.'

'You get the name of the company?' Eric asked curiously.

Jackie reached into the inside pocket of his windcheater and extracted a piece of paper. He passed it to Eric. 'I don't know what the end bit means.'

'Lincoln Shipping Pte Ltd,' Eric read out slowly. 'It's just the designation for a private limited company; that's how they register them in Singapore.'

'You ever heard of them?' Jackie Parton asked. There was something just a shade too casual in his tone.

Eric frowned, catching the reluctant lightness in the ex-jockey's tone. 'I can't say I have. Why do you ask?'

Jackie Parton grimaced. He glanced around the room, as though seeking some reason to say no more. When he spoke, the words almost struggled out. 'I just wondered. You see, Mr Ward, I wondered what you was up to ... asking me about the *Sierra Nova,* and Goldwaters, and the owners and all that. When the charterers were Lincoln Shipping.'

Puzzled, Eric shrugged. 'Lincoln Shipping. So?'

'I just wondered whether you knew that Lincoln Shipping was a subsidiary company. Wholly owned, it seems by Morcomb Estates.' He hesitated, licked his lips uncertainly. 'You know. Your wife's ... Mrs Ward's company.'

Eric stared at him, uncomprehendingly. 'Morcomb Estates is the holding company for a Singapore charterer...? You mean Anne's company was dealing through Goldwaters, in the charter arrangements for the *Sierra Nova?* What the hell? I don't understand...'

A fly buzzed noisily along the window, seeking egress to the sunshine beyond. A flight of ducks suddenly rose, clattering protest as they flew over the mediaeval bridge. Jackie Parton fiddled unhappily with his beer glass. 'I told you Paul

Sutherland went to Sedbergh, and Cambridge.'

Eric shook his head in irritation. 'Yes, you told me, but–'

'So did Jason Sullivan, Mr Ward. Sullivan went to Sedbergh School, same year as Sutherland. They were at Cambridge together. As we know, Sullivan read law, got called to the bar, became one of the youngest QCs. But it seems he never lost touch with his old mate, Paul Sutherland.' Jackie Parton paused thoughtfully. 'And Jason Sullivan ... he's on the board of Morcomb Estates, isn't he? Ever since you stood down yourself?'

Eric stared at the ex-jockey. He recalled his first meeting with Paul Sutherland, the hesitation the man had shown in proposing the retainer. A slow griping pain grew Eric's chest, a sickening feeling in his stomach. He clenched his fists; his mouth was dry with sudden anger. He knew now there would be no return to the apartment in Gosforth for him this evening. He had to pay a visit to Sedleigh Hall.

Chapter Eleven

The sun was low above the fells, causing Eric occasional problems as he made his way to the north west; the pale blue sky was studded with gold-edged dark clouds and as he drove along the long-shadowed, high-hedged roads he recalled that there were so many occasions when he had driven along these narrow back roads as the late

153

sun slanted across the hills, with a singing in his heart at the thought of returning to Sedleigh Hall, and Anne.

Now it was different.

The folds of the hills beyond Simonside still stretched ahead of him, green and brown and distant, faded blue; he crossed the winding Coquet, traversed narrow pack horse bridges, cut across the swards of common land, drove over the high fells and beyond the familiar craggy rock ledges, saw the harebell and wood sage still spread about him while above his head a solitary, wind-lifted, circling buzzard scanned the open moorland for prey. He skirted familiar clumps of woodland, relict oak, birch and ash which still sheltered deer and feral goats, and he recalled there had been times when this was nothing but pleasurable, but now there was a deep ache in his chest as he drove on towards the lands held by the Morcomb Estates, the inheritance of Anne's family, soon to be his family no more. Previously, over the years, he had always made his way back to Sedleigh with a lightness of mind, enjoying the relief from the problems he dealt with at the Quayside. Now, there was a grimness about him that he could not dispel as he finally breasted the hill and caught his first glimpse of the sprawling meadows, the low bottom land where the scattered beech trees reared their magnificent heads above the glittering, meandering stream, with the distant Cheviots as a backdrop, fading in the late afternoon haze.

He drove slowly up the long curving gravelled drive, his tyres rasping under the echoing trees. When he pulled up at the main entrance, he

154

became aware that a red Mercedes had been parked just to one side of the house, near the old stables. There was a bitterness on his tongue: Jason Sullivan was here with Anne at Sedleigh Hall. He grunted angrily to himself; but then subdued the anger with a cold deliberation – at least it meant he could kill two birds with one stone.

He left the Celica outside the main entrance and strode up the steps to the imposing entrance hall. He walked in, hesitated inside the great oak door, looked about him uncertainly, aware that this was no longer his home and then he heard someone at the top of the stairs. It was Anne. She caught sight of him and stopped for a moment, clearly shaken to see him standing there, un-expected, then she recovered her composure and came walking slowly down the broad curving staircase, one hand trailing on the dark oak banister rail, her eyes holding his challengingly.

'Eric. This is a surprise. You hadn't called to say you would be arriving.'

'I wasn't intending to come,' he replied grimly.

She stopped at the foot of the stairs, uncer-tainty in her eyes, one hand straying to her throat. 'Is there … is there something you wanted to pick up?' she asked hesitatingly. 'Is there some-thing you've forgotten?'

'I've taken all I want from Sedleigh Hall,' he replied coldly. The implication of his words hit home; she flinched and he half regretted the comment, but then he pushed the words aside, discarded the thought. There were other things he had to say. 'I see Jason Sullivan is here.'

She raised an eyebrow. There was a sudden

determination in her eyes that made him realise she recognised the need neither to apologise nor defend the presence of the man she had recruited as her legal adviser. In a cool tone, she explained, 'He came up to Sedleigh this morning. We had several business matters to discuss. So is it Jason you want to see?'

'In due course. But it can wait. It's you I want to talk to first of all.' He turned abruptly on his heel and marched into the library. She hesitated, then followed him, with a slow reluctant step. He closed the door behind her and watched her as she walked over to the window, stared out over the lawns, with the late afternoon sun gilding her hair, outlining the planes of her face. She had never been a beautiful woman but she had possessed for him an innate warmth, an attractiveness that was more than mere beauty; she was more mature now than the woman he had first fallen in love with; he had a brief, flashing glimpse in his mind of the first time he had seen Anne Morcomb, pacing down from Vixen Hill on the magnificent mare she rode... With an effort he cast the image and sentiment aside, obliterated it brutally.

'Did you enjoy the charity dinner the other evening?' she asked with a studied casualness that was somewhat belied by the tension in her back as she continued to look out over the meadows.

Taken aback, Eric frowned. 'Well enough.'

'I hear you didn't lack for company when you went home.'

'Who told you that?' Eric asked, irritated at being diverted from his purpose.

She sighed theatrically. 'Eric, you really must

156

know that on public occasions like charity dinners there are always watchful eyes, and spiteful tongues.' She turned slowly, eyed him carefully for a few moments. She was unable to suppress the hint of jealous resentment in her tone. 'So, who was she?'

'Someone I've come across professionally. A barrister. Sharon Owen.'

'Know her well?'

'Barely.'

'As barely,' she asked coolly, 'as you knew Sandra Vitali?' He had tried to forget that business; it was over a year ago, but now the mention of the call-girl's name brought up a brief, flashing image in his mind, the naked, lifeless body, green eyes vacant in death. He remembered how he had stood over her, covering the nakedness, trying to give back to her some of the dignity she had lost, and then he thrust the memory aside, anger bubbling in his chest. 'That's a cheap shot,' he muttered.

'We've never discussed it before,' Anne remarked coldly.

'In the same way that we've never discussed your relationship with Jason Sullivan, or what went on between you that time in Singapore,' he countered. It was a battle they had never fought openly, and yet it was what had destroyed their marriage. They had tried to paper over the doubts and the distrust, but the tension had remained there, simmering under the surface, slowly eroding their ability to live together, to compromise, to prevent the slow erosion of their marriage. And it was pointless now for one to try to wound the other, when irrevocable decisions had been made. As she stared at him, he saw the wavering uncertainty in her eyes and Eric knew that the realisation had come to her also. 'I don't think there's much point in continuing this,' she said slowly. 'But, from your attitude,' she suggested, 'it seems you've come to chide me about something.'

'Chide isn't quite the word I had in mind,' he replied. 'I want to talk to you about a retainer I've been given.'

'A retainer? Oh, it's business, then?' she asked carelessly, moving from the window to walk slowly along the side of the library table, looking up to the glass-fronted shelves ranged with the expensive, handsomely bound books over which he had browsed so many times.

'Goldwaters. They've paid me a considerable amount of money as a retainer, to act for them in a shipping matter.'

'So? Does that mean you're moving up-market in your clientele? Not before time, I would have thought.' She looked back over her shoulder at him, and raised her chin with an air of defiance.

Eric's tone was cold. 'I thought it was strange when they came to me. I took the retainer with a certain reluctance, because I couldn't really understand why they wanted me to act for them, when they had their own lawyers. Now, I've begun to realise why exactly they did approach me.'

'And why would that be?'

'It was you who put them up to it.'

'What makes you think that?' she asked guardedly.

'Don't put on that innocent air with me, Anne!

158

I know you better than that! They would never have made contact if you hadn't pushed them into making an approach to me.'

'That's not the way it was,' she flashed in sudden anger. 'But even if it was as you suggest, why are you complaining? They're a big firm; I would imagine it would have been a handsome retainer; why should I not recommend to them someone I know is a good lawyer, even if he is a damned stubborn one who's always refused to fulfil his own potential!'

Eric's anger matched her own. 'There's a bloody good reason why you shouldn't have recommended me. It's because you and I have different views about how I should run my professional life. And because I've made it absolutely clear that I don't want you interfering in that life. I'll go my own way, Anne, and I don't want you salving your own conscience by scattering handfuls of charitable seed in front of me, patronising me–'

'Conscience? What the hell do you mean, salving my conscience? I've done nothing to be ashamed of. And as for Goldwaters, I recommended you because I thought you could do a job for them, and because I thought it would help!'

'Don't you realise after all this time that I don't *want* your help?' Eric snapped. 'I thought I'd made that clear from the start. I didn't want your help and your influence all the years we've been married, and I certainly don't want them now.' He clenched his fists, anger rushing through his veins, and then suddenly he relaxed, the anger against her evaporating, as a feeling akin to despair came washing over him. He shook his head despondently. 'Can't you see, Anne, I just want to go my own way. It's better that the break is clean. I can't have you ... helping me, trying to build me a better practice...'

'But you're walking away from me, and Morcomb Estates, with virtually nothing, just because of your stubborn pride. I only thought ... this was a way in which I could make some amends at least...' She gave up, shaking her head in frustration. 'We've been over this time and again.'

'And this has got to be the *last* time,' he replied in grim determination. They stood there facing each other in a desperate silence: physically it was merely a short distance between them but it could have been a yawning gulf, emotionally. At last she nodded slowly. 'All right, Eric. I give up. Have it your own way. Stick to your mean little practice and throw away your professional skills on the mud flats of the Tyne. I'm sorry I interfered.'

She stood there, waiting. He was uncertain how to respond, with the anger shredding away from him in face of her capitulation. 'So, was it just your idea?' he asked after a while, curiously.

She hesitated, trailed uncertain fingers along the top of the polished mahogany library table at her side. 'More or less. There was a certain resistance, but I talked to Paul Sutherland at a dinner party he held, and I was able to persuade him that Goldwaters...'

'Are you sure that was the way it happened?' Eric queried, unable to keep the note of disbelief out of his tone.

'How do you mean?'

He noted the edge of evasiveness in her voice.

160

'What part did Jason Sullivan play in making the recommendation?'

Her glance hardened, her mouth tightened stubbornly. 'I see. We're going to drag up old enmities.'

'Not enmities, old realities,' he countered. 'I've tried to warn you in the past about Sullivan—'

'You let petty jealousies stand in the way of reasoned judgement, Eric. That's more like the truth of the matter.'

'That's not so. I've always thought he was the wrong kind of person for you to rely on. He's got a big reputation, but he's moved on the edge of a shady world—'

'*Shady?*' Her voice was raised in a flash of anger and contempt. 'He works on my boards as my legal adviser – because you eventually refused to do so – and he's been helpful in a number of business deals, arranged the affairs of Morcomb Enterprises with more skill and acumen than you ever demonstrated. And you of all people dare talk of shady activities, when your clients are mainly petty criminals and drop-outs, drug addicts and tearaways, who come from the dingy back streets of Newcastle and Shields, and the muckrakings of the lowest parts of the riverside! Jason's had the sense to make use of his background and connections, work in the right circles, order his professional life in areas where money can be made, civilised society enjoyed, polite conversation indulged in, whereas you... *Shady!*'

She was beside herself with fury, but the bitterness was churning in Eric's chest again as he rounded on her. 'There's not a world of difference between the activities of the people I have to

161

deal with, and the chicanery that whirls around the boardrooms. It's only a matter of degree, believe me, that, and the amounts of money involved. You forget, Anne, I worked in that world on your behalf for five years. And that was more than long enough. As for Jason Sullivan–'

'I hate having my name taken in vain.'

He was standing there in the doorway, a hard-edged smile on his lips. Tall, elegant, suave, and confident, Jason Sullivan carried his success with a light air. Fit from regular sessions of squash, as an old rugby blue at Cambridge and an honours man at the bar he had had the skills and connections to rise swiftly in his profession, taking silk at a young age. But he had moved away from practice in the courts of recent years. Keen grey eyes, fair hair that tended to flop in unruly fashion over his high forehead, finely chiselled nose – his looks drew the eyes of women in any social function he attended and his career concentration upon corporate law matters had persuaded Anne that he would be a good choice to represent her on the boards of some of the companies in the group holdings of Morcomb Estates. Now, he advanced into the room with a casual confidence, smiling at Anne. 'If this is a private conversation, of course, I'll make myself scarce. But since I did hear my name...'

He glanced towards Eric, a cold, glinting challenge in his eyes. The tigerish smile remained on his lips. Eric nodded slowly. 'I see no reason why you shouldn't be present when I warn Anne of the dangerous waters into which you seem to be taking her.'

'Me? Dangerous waters?' Sullivan laughed.

'Exciting corporate deeps maybe, but dangerous? What on earth are you talking about, Ward?'

Eric watched as Anne moved slightly, away from the table, to stand nearer to Sullivan. There was a tentative, hesitant air to her movements, but he was aware she was signalling something else too: she was aligning herself, if only sub-consciously, with her legal adviser against the man from whom she would soon be divorced. There was a cold knot in Eric's stomach. 'I've just remonstrated with Anne, about my being given a retainer by Paul Sutherland.'

Sullivan's grey eyes were amused. 'Ah. Then you and I, we find ourselves in accord for once, Ward. When Anne first mooted it, I told her I thought it was a bad idea too. But, you know Anne. Philanthropic as always. She went ahead with it anyway. Persuaded Paul that you could do a job for him.' He smiled reassuringly at her. 'Lame dogs and stiles and all that.'

Eric recognised the mockery, but kept his anger in check. 'You know Paul Sutherland well?'

'The director at Goldwaters? Of course. We went to school together. And university. We've always kept in touch. Even though years ago we went our separate ways, in business and pro-fessional terms.'

'But recently re-established business contact, it seems. Was it because of your connection with Sutherland that a link was established between Goldwaters and Lincoln Shipping?'

There was a short silence, while Sullivan ap-praised Eric coolly, considering his reply. At last, he commented airily, 'Business deals are struck with people one can trust, or where there is mutual respect and mutual interests. I would be the last to suggest that old boy networks, as they're called, play no part in business decisions, but that's the way the world works.'

'And it was you who actually set up Lincoln Shipping, wasn't it?'

Jason Sullivan glanced at Anne, smiled at her in reassurance. 'I'm not sure we should now be discussing the affairs of Morcomb Estates with you in the present...'

'We have nothing to hide from Eric,' Anne interrupted stiffly.

Sullivan gave a nod of graceful acquiescence. 'Well then, as you wish, Anne. I'm sure we all recall that unfortunate business over the timber licences, Ward, when Anne and I had to go to Singapore last year, to do the deal with Dato' Rashid and the Californians. It all went haywire, of course, but I was able to pick something up out of the rubble. We had already established a company to handle the timber concessions; we were able to change its name to Lincoln Shipping and alter the objectives and the memorandum of association—'

'And that was my decision,' Anne interrupted firmly. 'I looked at the possibilities, the chance to recoup some losses, the potential, the opportunity for further diversification for Morcomb Estates...'

'And Anne is the boss,' Sullivan grinned confidently 'But you seem to be suggesting that the ... ah ... investment by Morcomb Estates was an unwise one.'

'It is, in view of the fact that the company might be subjected to a criminal investigation,' Eric said sharply, nettled by Sullivan's cool arrogance.

Anne stared at him for several moments. Then, almost instinctively she moved even closer to Jason Sullivan, closing ranks, so her shoulder was actually touching his. 'This is insufferable, Eric! Making wild allegations simply because you don't approve of Jason–'

Eric's silence unnerved her, and the impact of his words suddenly got to her. She shot a quick glance at Sullivan, then looked back to Eric. 'Criminal investigation. What exactly is that supposed to mean?' she asked in edgy belligerence.

'Yes,' Sullivan said thoughtfully, his cold grey eyes appraising Eric. 'Perhaps you'd like to elucidate for us both.'

Eric was aware of the pulse beating angrily in his temple. He felt suddenly exposed, forced by his own irritation at their apparent closeness into indiscretion, betrayal of information given to him for other purposes. But he had gone too far to turn back now. 'Lincoln Shipping, the Singapore based subsidiary of Morcomb Enterprises Ltd, is involved with the chartering of a freighter called the *Sierra Nova.*'

'So?' Anne asked irritably.

'That ship itself is currently being held at North Shields, under arrest.'

'There're often commercial issues,' Sullivan said carelessly, waving a dismissive hand, 'document-ation not strictly in line, previous charterers making absurd claims, demurrage, cargo insurance–'

'This isn't a matter of commercial insurance claims,' Eric interrupted. 'Not when the IMB are involved.'

165

'Who?' Anne asked uncertainly.

'The International Maritime Bureau,' Eric snapped. He stared at the couple facing him, and suddenly knew that it was useless, trying to drive a wedge between them, persuade her that Sullivan was unreliable. She would put it down to bitterness, and recall all the things that had been said, and left unsaid. Defeated, he felt his visit to Sedleigh Hall had been pointless, inadvisable, a foolish attempt to assuage the anger that raged in him. Anne had her own legal counsel, and it was clear from her stance just who she would be relying upon for support. He turned to go, to leave the place he had called home for so many years. 'Perhaps Mr Sullivan will explain to you all about it. I'll see my own way out. I know it well enough.'

'Eric...' she began falteringly, then fell silent.

He made his way out back into the echoing hall, and down the steps to his car for the long despondent drive south to Newcastle.

Chapter Twelve

They had arranged to meet at the Malmaison Hotel. The proposed rendezvous, close to Wesley Square and the Millennium Bridge on the newly developed riverside was a surprise to Eric: the fashionable, sophisticated five star luxury of the hotel, which had been redeveloped from the towering warehouse of the old Co-operative Society Building seemed hardly Charlie Spate's style. Moreover, it was a lunch engagement, and Eric was unaware that Spate enjoyed such surroundings normally for meetings with his informants. For that was how Eric now thought of himself, with a degree of dissatisfaction. Informant to DCI Charlie Spate. It was not a position he considered enviable.

Eric made his way through the automatic swing doors, past reception and turned to climb the stairs to the bar and brasserie on the floor above. When he entered he could see that Charlie Spate was already ensconced in one of the smart chairs in the bar: he wore a freshly laundered dark suit, crisp white shirt, dark green tie and a self-satisfied expression. Coffee had already been served to him in a silvered pot, along with a white-napkinned salver, delicate china side plate with oatmeal and chocolate chip biscuits placed beside a small blue table lamp. 'My favourites,' Spate explained, gesturing to the biscuits as Eric approached. 'I got a sweet tooth, did you know that?'

'I didn't. I always thought your teeth were for sinking into villains.' Eric sat down, looked about him at the discreetly lit lounge, with its rich plum-coloured carpeting and matching chairs. DCI Spate had stationed himself beside a mirrored pillar; there were only three other people in the room, dark-suited businessmen, possibly lawyers, Eric guessed, discussing matters with clients before hearings. He glanced around at the décor: art deco posters, black and white prints, each with an accompanying quotation. Spate caught the glance and snorted. 'I like the one over there. *The brain is a wonderful organ – it starts working when*

167

you get up in the morning and doesn't stop till you get to the office. It applies to a number of people I know at Ponteland.'

Eric sat down across the table from Spate. 'This one of your usual haunts, then?'

Charlie Spate shook his head, ignored the irony. He sipped his coffee with noisy satisfaction. 'Not my idea, meeting you here. Some other people will be joining us shortly. There's a private room booked for lunch.'

'So that's why the sharp suit. High flying.'

Spate eyed him sardonically. 'Quite your style, not so long ago, I hear. When you were acting for your wife on the board of those merchant bankers Martin and Channing, there must have been plenty of opportunities for lunches at places like this. Brasseries, with a *salon prive* dedicated to wine and a background of soft French love songs.'

'I walked away from all that,' Eric reminded him.

'Can't imagine why,' Spate sniffed, looking about him in appreciation. 'Not a bad way to live. Now if it had been me–'

'It wasn't,' Eric interrupted shortly. 'Anyway, you wanted to see me. You got my phone call–'

'About Patsy Gullane, yes. Bit late though, wasn't it?' Spate complained. 'I mean, she was already in police custody by then. Her body, anyway.'

Eric shrugged. 'I wondered about making the call at all. But you'd asked me to find out what I could. So, even though the police had already recovered her body from Border Mires, I thought I'd better get in touch. And give you Billy Leven's name.'

168

'Billy Leven, yeah...' Charlie Spate munched on a chocolate chip cookie reflectively. He wiped some crumbs from the jacket of his newly pressed suit, glanced appreciatively at himself in the mirrored pillar, and sat back in the armchair. 'We looked him up. Talked to a few people in his old haunts out west. Wild colonial boy. Trouble with shooters, over in Liverpool. Served some time. Quite a lad. But kept his red head down, more or less, since he came to Tyneside. You tell me he was Patsy Gullane's minder.'

'Lover, I understand,' Eric corrected him. 'It seems they were shacked up together.'

'We got people out looking for him.'

'But not too seriously, I hear,' Eric suggested.

There was a pause. Something glittered briefly in Charlie Spate's eyes as he looked at Eric. 'It's been a while since you left the force, Ward. Things have changed. But some things never change.'

'Like office politics?'

'You could say that.'

'Do you think that Gullane's murder was in some way linked to the killing of the crewman, off the *Sierra Nova?*' Eric asked.

'It's a line of enquiry we're pursuing,' Spate mumbled unconvincingly. 'But there's also a line of thinking that maybe this Gullane thing, it was just a sex killing. I mean, with her history—'

'My information is she was no longer on the game. What do forensics say? Was she sexually assaulted?'

'Hey, come on, you know that some perverts get off without actually doing any fumbling,' Spate protested half-heartedly. 'Anyway, I've not

169

seen any reports from the labs yet.'

It bore out what Jackie Parton had hinted at to Eric. Somehow, the pressure wasn't on, in the murder enquiry of the deck hand called Edwards, and now the killing of the ex-whore called Patsy Gullane. It was strange; and it would be down to office politics, of some kind.

Charlie Spate was watching him with narrowed, appraising eyes as he finished off the remains of his biscuit. He wiped the back of his hand across his mouth. 'So, I'm curious. What made you change your mind in the end?'

'About what?'

Spate grunted sardonically. 'Don't come that with me, Ward. You gave me and Chris Michaels the old heave-ho when we came to your office; and when I phoned you later you still weren't exactly falling over yourself to help. But you did so, eventually. You phoned me back with the Gullane information. And you gave me Leven's name. So what made you change your mind? No longer pleading confidentiality and all that sort of crap.'

Eric hesitated. He had been over the matter in his mind continuously. In the end he had decided to co-operate with Spate for several reasons – because a murder enquiry overrode his conscience about disclosing commercial matters, because Anne needed protection from herself, because he disliked Sullivan and didn't trust him. And because, he was forced to admit, he wanted to settle a debt once and for all. 'I had a monkey on my back,' he said shortly.

'Me, you mean.' Charlie Spate smiled in lupine satisfaction. 'I take no offence. But let's get something clear, Ward, the Gullane twitch doesn't get you off any hooks with me. I could have caused you big problems a year ago, but I stayed my hand. You could have got struck off, if I'd opened my mouth. But to make us even, to settle the score, you got to do more than just tell me it was Patsy Gullane that you saw that day – now she's dead. And naming Billy Leven doesn't amount to the necessary icing on the cake. You got to follow through with the other information you hinted at. Concerning the *Sierra Nova*. And that's why you been called here to a meeting today.'

'And that's what settles everything between us,' Eric insisted.

Charlie Spate picked up another biscuit, and nodded. 'If you come through with what we want, fair enough.' He dipped the oatmeal biscuit into his coffee and bit hurriedly at it as it softened. 'I'm still interested in your ethics, though. I don't expect you'll tell me, but I wonder how you square this with your professional conscience.'

'That's my problem,' Eric muttered.

'Yeah. Though from my position, it seems to me your conscience, your professional ethics, they've got sort of battered over this last year or so. You was always regarded as straight ... and now, well, I look at this biscuit and I think...'

A black-waistcoated waiter had moved forward to stand obsequiously at Eric's shoulder. 'May I get you some coffee, sir?'

Before Eric could answer Charlie Spate waved him away. 'Don't bother, son. No time. We'll be moving upstairs in a few minutes.'

'Who will we be joining?' Eric asked.

171

'One guy you know. Chris Michaels.' Charlie Spate appeared to find the name distasteful. 'Couple of other people he's bringing along. You'll get introduced.'

'IMB people?'

'You'll find out,' Spate said. He glanced at his watch, finished his coffee and rose to his feet. He glanced at his reflection in the mirrored pillar, straightened his green tie. 'Like right now.'

The young waiter hovered; Spate dismissed him grandly, informing him everything would be put on the bill for the private party upstairs, and led the way to the lift. They rode to the third floor, walked along the thickly carpeted corridor to the room at the corner of the building. Spate marched in without ceremony and looked about him.

'Hah!' he sneered. 'Small but perfectly formed!' There were seven seats ranged around the table, already laid for lunch in the narrow meeting room. Their polished leather coverings gleamed blackly, in sharp contrast to the perfect white of the tablecloth. The wine glasses sparkled; Charlie Spate picked up one and flicked his finger against it. The musical note pleased him. 'Nice,' he said admiringly. He walked across to the drinks cabinet in the corner of the room, selected a bottle of expensive gin and helped himself liberally, topped it with tonic water. 'If this was a really class place, there'd be a waiter here to do this,' he suggested. 'Or maybe it's the bloody security Chris Michaels wants to maintain. You want something?'

'I'll have a Perrier,' Eric said. He had a feeling he might need to keep a clear head, and avoid

172

being trapped into making admissions or betraying information that might be against his professional conscience.

'Suit yourself,' Spate shrugged. 'I just feel when you're in Rome, you take what you can grab, and enjoy it. Here's to a successful meeting.'

As he spoke, the door opened and a small group of men came in silently. Charlie Spate stiffened, as the first man remarked, 'I see you've made a start already, Spate.'

'Yes, sir,' Spate replied, permitting no hint of apology in his tone. 'But with our guest already here, Mr Ward, one has to be hospitable. After all, he's not here under any duress, is he? Mr Ward, may I introduce you to Mr Dawes, Deputy Chief Constable.'

'We've not met before, Ward, but I've heard of you,' Dawes said gripping Eric's extended hand firmly. 'You were one of us, at one time, I hear.'

'A long time since, sir.'

Dawes was turning, to introduce the others. 'Chris Michaels you've already met, I understand. This is Mr Pendragon, from the Home Office...'

Eric nodded and shook hands with the pinstriped, smooth-faced civil servant and then was introduced to a heavily built, bald man with wary eyes. 'Mr Schwartz, liaison officer from Interpol... And this is our honoured guest, Mr Cheung, from the Chinese Embassy.'

The short, smiling, immaculately-suited Chinese man with the deceptively innocent moon face bowed in slight deference and extended his hand; the skin was soft, the grip inconsequential. 'My friends call me Henry,' he informed Eric. 'So

173

much less formal than Mr Cheung, don't you agree?'

They moved forward to the drinks cabinet as Charlie dispensed liquor; Henry Cheung accepted a stiff glass of brandy, Dawes took a gin and tonic of a strength similar to Charlie Spate's, Schwartz settled for whisky while Chris Michaels pointed to a bottle of rum. When his glass was half filled with the dark liquid he turned, raised his glass of rum in Eric's direction. 'Got to keep up traditions and expectations,' he suggested. 'Let's hope we have a productive meeting, in the interests of the service, and everyone here.' He kept his eyes fixed on Eric as he did so, and there was a hint of a threat in his glance. He was an unforgiving man, Eric decided, who had not forgotten the previous rebuff.

Pendragon had taken a glass of dry sherry. He stood beside Eric, smiling faintly. 'As a representative of the Home Office, I too must maintain appearances. We are well known to exist on sherry and tea.' He presented a neat, ascetic appearance, narrow-featured, dark greying hair neatly parted, a thin mouth that would rarely display real humour or pleasure but a man to whom dissembling would come naturally. He would be someone who could keep a secret, and retained many; a dangerous man in some ways, with access to powerful people. He leaned one shoulder casually against the wall as he chatted to Eric, asking him about his practice, and his background. Eric knew Pendragon wasn't really interested: he would have already been briefed with all that was necessary to know.

The others stood talking, sipping their drinks, indulging in meaningless polite chatter, until

DCC Dawes suddenly suggested, 'Shall we sit down, gentlemen? I know we all have other commitments, and we should get down directly to business. I've arranged for lunch to be served immediately: we can talk as we eat.'

They took the seats he suggested. Eric found himself next to Charlie Spate, opposite the Australian IMB inspector and the moon-faced Chinese man. Dawes sat at the head of the table, Pendragon beside him, Schwartz at the far end. Two silent waiters glided in and served them with crab salad. When they had closed the door behind them, and Charlie was attacking his crab, the deputy chief constable, taking the chairmanship as a matter of right, suggested, 'Perhaps we might make a start with your bringing us up to date, Michaels.' He glanced stonily at Charlie Spate, already tucking hungrily into his crab, and then turned to Michaels as the Australian began to speak.

'We've been maintaining regular contact with Interpol through Mr Schwartz here, and operations are now poised to commence in Hamburg, Marseilles and Barcelona. The final link in the European chain lies here with us. The matter of the *Sierra Nova* is still in hand, and I hope that in due course Mr Ward might be able to give us some information in that respect. Meanwhile, matters have progressed at speed. Just recently, evidence has reached us that the freighter *Shinjitsu Maru*, which we believe was previously known as the *Kefalonia Wind*, and before that *The Alexandros*, was recently detained in the Yangtze River. Now the last occasion on which such a ship was detained, it would seem that a Chinese patrol boarded the freighter, but it was the legitimate crewmen – who had been held captive by the pirates – who ended up being accused of smuggling. The pirates themselves sort of faded away out of the picture. Not for the first, and only time.'

He fixed the man from the Chinese embassy with a glittering challenge in his eyes. Henry Cheung spread his hands, smiled faintly, but made no immediate reply.

'They were held in custody for a month, before being released,' Michaels went on. 'As I said, the piratical group disappeared. They have not been traced, although one of them – a man we later held in the capture of the *Pulau Tengah,* off Johor – has been able to give us some information.' He stopped, and looked again at Henry Cheung, and now the accusation was clear in his glance, and in the tone of his voice.

The Chinese embassy official did not seem disturbed. He pushed aside the plate of crab, which he had hardy touched. He folded plump, complacent hands in front of him. 'It is obviously incumbent on me to offer an explanation. But first, I feel we should all be aware of the position of the Chinese government on this issue. China is a signatory to the Rome Convention of 1988, and specifically to Article 10. This Article obliges all signatory countries to submit piracy cases for prosecution. This we adhere to, as a matter of policy and of principle.'

Pendragon leaned forward, the lean fingers of his left hand caressing his cheek thoughtfully. 'That is clearly understood by Her Majesty's

Government. But there is a certain ... ah ... confusion at the Home Office – and we are in close liaison with the Foreign Office on this matter also – as to what exactly happened in the case mentioned by Mr Michaels.'

There was something underlying his tone which Eric could not latch on to: it was a mixture of warning and persuasion, steel under the soft, caressing glove.

Henry Cheung waved his hands deprecatingly. 'While I cannot speak for my government openly on such matters, now that we are here among friends, and since we are here with common objectives – namely, the ending of this terrible trade – I can give my personal opinion about these ... histories. It is of course a matter of record that my government has always vehemently denied any involvement in the actions of what we may describe as certain rogue elements in the Chinese military, the police and the customs and excise.' He looked around him, dark eyes rounded innocently in his broad face. 'We have come across instances even of pirates posing as Chinese naval personnel when they board these ships. There was the case of the cargo ship carrying durian timber to Australia, for instance ... the pirates were dressed in Chinese naval uniforms. So you will appreciate that these are matters of great difficulty to deal with. But, in addition, you must understand, gentlemen, that in China now we are seeing days of great change. You have a saying ... Rome cannot be built in a day. Compare Rome with China.' He smiled deprecatingly. 'Ours is a much greater task, is it not?'

'What of the *Shinjitsu Maru?*' Chris Michaels demanded roughly. He was the player here who pressed issues, Eric concluded, while others like Pendragon would mollify, soften, persuade, observe the niceties. They were taking part in an elaborate political dance, with his own position in the lineup not yet resolved in his own mind. The Chinese embassy official seemed unperturbed by Michaels's directness, but he hooded his eyes, inspecting his barely touched plate. 'The matter has already been dealt with.'

'How do you mean?' Pendragon asked softly. 'In what manner, dealt with?'

'I have received official information this morning,' Henry Cheung replied, after a slight pause. 'The thirteen pirates who were apprehended on the *Shinjitsu Maru,* they were all executed three days ago. They had been convicted under Chinese law of the murder of the twenty crew members of the vessel. The evidence against them was irrefutable. They had even been so foolish as to take photographs of the celebrations in which they drunkenly indulged, after killing the crew.' He eyed the glass in front of him with an ironic air. 'It would seem that numerous bottles of brandy had been consumed. A Chinese vice, I fear.'

'And the *Shinjitsu Maru?*' Pendragon asked.

'I am also able to confirm that documentation seized shows quite clearly that the cargo ship was indeed one of your so-called phantoms. The pirates had seized it outside Hong Kong waters, dressed as Chinese officials. A heinous offence. For which they paid with their lives.'

Chris Michaels was clearly angry. 'Execution?

Why the hell didn't–'

Pendragon stopped him in his tracks, with a raised hand. 'I don't think we need concern ourselves any longer with the *Shinjitsu Maru*. Quite clearly, the Chinese government, within its own jurisdiction, has acted as it thinks fit, and I am sure we are all grateful that steps are being taken to eradicate a problem that affects us all in the international shipping community of nations. What is more important, to us here right now, is what information can be provided to us in respect of the European end of the organisation's activities.'

There was a discreet tapping on the door, the waiters entered, and cleared away the plates. The small group sat in silence. Charlie Spate glanced expectantly at Eric, and drummed his fingers on the tablecloth in front of him, a slow dance of impatience. The man from Interpol sat stolidly, without expression. Wine was poured, a choice of Merlot or Chenin; a fish course was placed before them but Eric was barely interested in the turbot on his plate. Pressure was being placed on the Chinese embassy official, that was clear: it was almost palpable, with Schwartz's silence, Pendragon's insouciance barely covering the steel in his voice, and the openly expressed anger in the features of Chris Michaels. They wanted the co-operation of China in the suppression of the piracy ring; Eric suspected that there would be a quid pro quo. Henry Cheung had been ordered by his masters to co-operate with the IMB, and Pendragon's presence meant there would be some advantage offered as a result by Her Majesty's Government. What had he seen in the press recently ... a trade agreement due to be signed?

The turbot also remained untouched in front of the man from the Chinese embassy. When the waiters had left the room, he sighed. 'Before the pirates themselves were executed, and before the reactionary criminals who had given them the opportunity to operate in Chinese waters had suffered a similar fate, my government was able to obtain considerable information regarding the operation of the organisation which supports this activity. Some of this information has already been transmitted to the countries interested...'

Schwartz spoke for the first time. 'That is correct.' His English was slightly accented, his tone clipped. 'I can confirm that Interpol has received documentation and statements and these have been passed on to the relevant authorities in London, Hamburg, Marseilles and Barcelona.'

'You, Mr Michaels, are concerned particularly about the *Sierra Nova*.' Cheung continued with a faint smile. 'We are now able to confirm that it has indeed been operating as a mother ship.'

DCC Dawes leaned forward, frowning. 'What exactly do you mean by that?'

Chris Michaels intervened, took the opportunity to explain. 'The way these guys operate is well known to us at the IMB. The contracted shipping agent – usually in Singapore – gets hold of all the necessary details regarding a particular freighter's cargo, destination, route and crew. Within the industry it's pretty common practice to change crew at various points during a voyage. At one of these changes a new crew member would be planted on the targeted ship by the organisation, and given a cellular phone.' He paused, glanced at Charlie Spate. 'That's how we managed to put one of our own people on board the *Sierra Nova*.'

Eric was aware of Charlie Spate shifting uncomfortably in his seat. He muttered something under his breath; it sounded like a muffled obscenity.

'Once aboard, the pirate contact keeps in touch with the shipping agent, giving him exact references as to where the ship is to be located at any precise point in the voyage. When it gets close to a specific area – like the Malacca Straits, or certain locations in the South China Sea – where the pirates operate, an attack is launched, by way of a heavily armed small group of men, on a fast launch. But once they've taken over the ship they still need support, and that's where a ship like the *Sierra Nova* comes in. She acts as a mother ship, on hand to provide the pirates with logistical backup – paint to recolour the hijacked victim, bogus registration documents, new flags, and maybe additional weaponry.' He grunted in disgust. 'In effect, the victim ship doesn't stand a chance. Once these guys are on board, that's it. You don't argue with them. You give them what they want.'

'But is there no security about these voyages?' Dawes asked in an incredulous tone. 'No attempt to prepare the crew against boarding?'

'The shipping world is a small one,' Michaels said coldly, his eyes flickering from Dawes, to Pendragon and on to Henry Cheung, as Schwartz nodded in silent agreement. 'Everything about a ship has to be documented – its course, its cargo, its destination. But the people who control the

181

pirates, they have learned to work from the inside, passing information onto the pirate gangs. And when the attack happens, it's usually when the ship is at its most vulnerable. When it's at anchor.'

'Why not just arm the crew, fight off these bastards?' Spate asked belligerently.

Michaels made no attempt to disguise the open contempt in his voice. 'The options have been discussed endlessly, believe me, mate. We've talked of defensive measures, fire-hoses, high-powered searchlights, barbed wire, reinforced cabin locks and windows. You think any of that would deter these killers? As to arming the crew, can you imagine it? Most of these deck crews are multi-national, cheap, hired labour, on freighters carrying aluminium ingots to South Korea, timber to Malaysia, kerosene, oil, gas. They're deck hands, not SAS trained specialists, for God's sake! You put AK47s in their hands – do you think they'd know how to use them? Besides, why should they want to put their lives at risk to save a cargo for some shipping contractor they don't even know, and who pays them bottom wages at that?'

'Perhaps we should move on,' Pendragon suggested in emollient tones. 'To get back to this ... local situation. The *Sierra Nova*.' He turned to fix a piercing glance upon Eric. 'Perhaps it's time to hear from Mr Ward.'

Chapter Thirteen

It was the moment Eric had been dreading. Since his meeting with Jackie Parton he had spent several sleepless nights over the question of how much he should divulge to Charlie Spate. Armed with the information given to him by the ex-jockey Eric had carried out his own research, both at Companies House in Cardiff and the Companies Registry in Singapore. He had also been talking to a number of people he himself had known over the years, and who might provide some kind of insight, some kind of background to the questions that were being raised. He'd even sought out Posh Harry himself, to get a few more details than Jackie Parton had been able to provide. Posh Harry had been amenable, after a few drinks.

And even when he had made his final decision to phone Charlie Spate Eric had remained uncertain of just how far to go. But now he was facing the issue head on. He looked around at the group of expectant faces in the meeting room at the Malmaison Hotel.

'You will appreciate, I'm sure,' he said quietly, 'that I find myself in a difficult position. As Mr Michaels and DCI Spate are already aware I have been in receipt of information which is rightly owned by one of my clients, and to that extent I feel unable, in my capacity as a lawyer, to give you free and fully open access to that information.

However, I have made various enquiries, and in so far as the information does not radically affect my relationship with my client and my legal obligations towards them I'm prepared to co-operate with your own investigations.'

'Spoken like a true shyster,' Charlie Spate muttered sarcastically. Dawes glared at him, then nodded to Eric to proceed.

'Chris Michaels had asked me to try to find out who owned the *Sierra Nova*,' Eric continued. 'I am still in no position to advise you. What I can disclose is that, in my view, my clients have not knowingly proceeded along any culpable lines in this business.'

Chris Michaels snorted, and sat back in his chair with a cynical sigh of disbelief. Eric ignored him. 'It may well be that they have been caught up in a criminal conspiracy of some kind, but they have not done so knowingly. They are a respectable firm of insurance brokers, with various shipping interests–'

'We're talking about Goldwaters here,' Chris Michaels interjected.

Eric stared at him coldly. 'If you're so certain of that I can't imagine why you've been asking me to disclose the identity of my clients. However, I have already spoken to my clients and advised them of the interest aroused in their activities, and my contact – and contract – with them has now been ended.'

The telephone conversation had been bitter. Paul Sutherland had been furious when he received the cheque from Eric, repaying the retainer, and there had been a blazing row between the two men, with Sutherland warning that if Eric did not change his mind he would see his practice go down in flames. It was clear he had been forewarned by Jason Sullivan, but Eric had finally given him the assurance that he would not compromise Goldwaters, while insisting that it was his duty to co-operate with police enquiries. Sutherland's response had been brief, explicit and obscene before he crashed down the telephone.

'My clients have been involved with the insuring and chartering of the *Sierra Nova* in the full belief that they were dealing with a legitimate business activity. I was engaged by them to determine the legal grounds on which the freighter was being held at North Shields, and to advise whether an early release could be obtained in view of the further chartering that was available to the ship.'

'Once she'd been chartered and set sail again,' Michaels interjected emphatically, 'she'd have done a bloody disappearing act again.'

'That may well be so,' Eric replied coolly. 'But that was something my clients would have known nothing about. Indeed, it seems that their involvement was, shall we say, at some arm's length. From the enquiries I've made, I've come to the conclusion that it was their name which was being used, in order to give cover and credence to someone else.'

'How do you mean?' Dawes asked, leaning forward in his chair.

'My clients have a sound reputation on Tyneside, and in the Baltic shipping area generally,' Eric explained. 'Their name could provide good cover for a smaller, less well known operation of shorter longevity in the business. Maybe someone tied in with the operations you've been describing.'

'So who were your clients providing the cover for?' Charlie Spate asked.

'A company based in Singapore,' Eric replied slowly. 'Registered in that city state as Lincoln Shipping Pte Ltd.'

Schwartz raised his heavy head and glanced at Michaels, who nodded slowly. 'The Lion City again.'

Pendragon sipped at the glass of white wine in front of him, and said almost casually, 'I suppose you've been able to obtain some information about this company ... which does in fact appear among our list of suspects, though it makes no appearance in the documentation that was discovered aboard the *Sierra Nova,* if my information is correct.'

Eric nodded. 'I've undertaken a full company search, and I've also made other enquiries here, and in Singapore and London. During my time as a board member of Martin and Channing, I made a number of contacts...' He hesitated; further details were unnecessary. 'Lincoln Shipping has offices in the Asia Insurance Building, near Anson Road in Singapore. It's a small office; it employs only three staff. Since the company is only fourteen months old it has not yet filed any annual accounts, so it is impossible to determine what volume of business has in reality been undertaken by the company.'

'Are you suggesting it's a fly by night operation?' Dawes enquired, puzzled.

Eric shrugged. 'Impossible to say, until its books are exposed to audit. Their end of period accounts will have to be submitted in four months time, under Singaporean law. But from what I can gather from contacts in the financial press, it seems to have picked up a certain amount of credibility in Singapore itself. Which means that its capital base must be considerable. In the Lion City,' he added dryly, as he caught Henry Cheung's eye, 'money talks.'

'All right,' Chris Michaels intervened, 'so you've come up with Lincoln Shipping as a go-between charterer, which has been using Gold ... sorry your clients,' he sneered, 'as a front. Just how did they achieve that, as a new, unknown company, dealing with a respectable, long-established firm?'

Eric hesitated. 'I think it was based upon a personal relationship between one of the directors of my client company, and a director of Lincoln Shipping.'

'The old boy network?' Pendragon murmured, smiling slightly.

'Precisely.'

'Names?' Schwartz asked peremptorily.

Eric held the gaze of the man from Interpol for several seconds. He reached down beside his chair for the briefcase he had deposited there, opened it and extracted a slim folder. He passed it to the deputy chief constable. 'I've stated there all I've been able to find out about Lincoln Shipping, together with the names of directors of the company – much of which is in the public domain, of course – and a copy of their memorandum of association, which described their proposed

187

activities. As for the ownership ... the shareholding would seem to be in the hands of nominees. As for the board of directors, you will see among them three names, all Singaporean nationals. But they are of course holding on behalf of other persons.'

'Shadow directors? Such as?' Pendragon asked, his predatory eyes greedily fixed on the file Dawes was inspecting.

'Simon Tan,' the deputy chief constable read from Eric's notes. 'And Lord Millay; Sir Everett Crane ... who also appear on the list of board members.'

'Lending an air of respectability,' Pendragon murmured. 'They're known to be somewhat penurious, and prepared to lend their names for an appropriate reward. Cannon fodder.'

'And Jason Sullivan QC,' Dawes added.

Charlie Spate turned his head slowly to give Eric a long, contemplative look.

'I suspect that Sullivan will be holding his shares,' Eric explained woodenly, 'and his place on the board, in a representative capacity. He will in fact hold a controlling interest in Lincoln Shipping as a result.'

'And just who is he representing?' Schwartz demanded.

'A company called Morcomb Enterprises Ltd, which itself is a subsidiary of Morcomb Estates plc. A public limited company, whose funds have been used to float Lincoln Shipping, through Morcomb Enterprises, as a commercial investment in Singapore.'

Charlie Spate licked his lips wolfishly. 'And Morcomb Estates is owned lock, stock and barrel by your wife, I believe?'

The silence was long, and profound. Pendragon's eyes were fixed on Eric; there was nothing to be read in his glance. A slight smile played around Charlie Spate's mouth and suspicion was stamped on Chris Michaels's features. Only Dawes seemed unmoved by the announcement; he continued to sift through the information in the folder in front of him. At last, he said, 'Morcomb Estates is a well known company in the north east. And well regarded. Never been in any sort of trouble, as far as I've heard. The fact it's your wife's company ... what do you make of all this, Mr Ward?'

Eric hesitated. 'I ... I've taken the opportunity to discuss the matter briefly, with my wife. I'm quite certain in my own mind that she is not aware–'

'Everyone around you seems to be blinded by innocent ignorance,' Chris Michaels sneered.

Eric ignored the interruption. 'Morcomb Enterprises Ltd had established a Singapore based company over a year ago, to deal with timber licences from Malaysia. The venture fell through. So it was then proposed that the company should change its name, change its objectives, and enter the chartering business. Singapore has always seen itself as the shipping hub of the world. My wife ... she had regarded this as a commercial opportunity, put to her by her legal adviser, Jason Sullivan. She had been persuaded that this was a way of cutting losses, and entering a new field of commercial opportunity.'

'Chartering phantom ships,' Michaels cut in coldly.

189

'My wife wasn't to know that.'

'But her legal adviser...?' Pendragon prompted.

Eric was silent for a few moments. He thought back to Sullivan's sneering, confident arrogance. 'I don't know. That's for others to discover. But certainly he advised her on the business opportunity, and he made the relevant contact with a personal acquaintance in my client firm, to provide cover and credibility to Lincoln Shipping in the chartering of the *Sierra Nova*.'

Pendragon inspected his wine glass closely, as though it held the answer to all his questions. 'Jason Sullivan... The name is one I've come across before, somewhere...'

Eric hesitated. 'He was brought up before the Benchers of his Inn last year. His conduct was investigated over a matter involving certain insurance contracts. A ship called the *Princess Eugenie*. He was cleared, but with a warning, I understand.' Pendragon raised his eyebrows thoughtfully, and nodded. 'Yes, I seem to recall... Well, Mr Ward, that is all most fascinating.' He glanced around him reflectively. 'I'm sure my colleagues here will be interested in pursuing these matters, following the avenues you seem to have opened to us. This is all most public-spirited of you...' He turned back to Eric and smiled. 'Most public spirited, and we appreciate the ... ah ... personal problems that might have had to be overcome in disclosing these facts to us.' He turned his head slightly, to fix Henry Cheung with his gaze. 'I think that brings us back to our Chinese friends,' he suggested.

The man from the Chinese embassy placed his fingers together, tapping them slightly in a thoughtful way. 'I have been interested to hear Mr Ward speaking. He has confirmed certain information that has fallen into our hands, and so it is now possible, I feel, to place all cards on the table. I understand that the IMB has made the necessary arrangements elsewhere in Europe?'

Chris Michaels nodded assent. 'Marseilles, Hamburg, Barcelona.'

'The South East Asian centres will also be targeted, with the full co-operation of my government,' Cheung nodded. 'Then it remains only for us to deal with the United Kingdom operations.'

'Which is why we are here,' DCC Dawes intoned.

The man from the Chinese embassy sighed. 'It is a personal sadness to me that so many of my own race are so deeply involved in these activities. We Chinese, we have only two major vices – drinking and gambling. Perhaps you find that surprising, but it is so. And within the sphere of gambling, many risks are sometimes taken, and much money involved. One of such gambles would seem to have involved the *Sierra Nova*. We know that she is a mother ship, one of the fleet of phantoms. And her detention at North Shields has caused considerable consternation among certain groups here in the UK. Not least, that group based in Manchester, under the control of a gentleman called Philip Ong ... also known as Chang Lee Ong.' He smiled in deprecation. 'So many of us adopt Western names, to make life easier...'

Chris Michaels leaned forward purposefully. 'Philip Ong is the UK based organiser of the syndicate?'

'He is a man of many talents,' Cheung assured him. 'He is a British national, of course, but is multi-lingual and much travelled. I have no doubt that he has appeared on the fringe of a number of illegal activities...'

Schwartz nodded. 'His name is on our data-bases, and has been circulated from time to time, but nothing has been placed to his name, that national police forces could proceed on.'

Cheung smiled complacently, glancing at Pendragon. 'I believe we can say that times are now changing. In view of the new relationships that are being established between our governments, at the highest level, we are now able to make available to you certain ... information that has come into our possession, along the Pacific Rim and in the South China Sea, that can place our acquaintance Mr Ong at the edge of a web of deceit and criminal activity that will interest us all. Not just Mr Michaels and the IMB, but the police forces in the north and...' His gaze slipped from Dawes to Pendragon. '...and might assist in government policies also.'

Dawes cleared his throat in anticipation. 'Just what are we talking about here?'

'From information we have been able to obtain from our expatriates – who still have families in China, of course – it would seem that Mr Ong is what you call a linchpin in a group of Asian businessmen who have established a ring of considerable power in the north. Does one have a linchpin in a ring? Ah, no matter, your English language... These people are considerable players in the supply and distribution of drugs; they have local arrangements with northern businessmen for the import of Nepalese and Somalian prostitutes; they organise a considerable trade in the smuggling of cheap alcohol from Europe into Britain; they use a front of legitimate business enterprises such as long distance haulage for distribution of food-stuffs, to cover the insertion of considerable numbers of Afghan, Pakistani and Asian economic immigrants into the British black economy. We have evidence to show, for instance, that they have agents in some of the more remote Chinese villages, who make arrangements for men to be transported here where they disappear, and work as sweated labour to pay back the so-called costs of their journey. Yes, I think that it was a mistake on Mr Ong's part, if one thinks about it.'

'Mistake?' Pendragon queried.

Cheung smiled faintly. 'To extend his operations, to link up with the piracy syndicate; to persuade his colleagues to get involved with the business of phantom ships. It has brought international wrath down upon his head – and that of this group. Now, it is possible that they will all suffer for his foolishness. If only he had been less ambitious, and remained content with his localised criminal activities, he might have been untroubled...'

Until someone else stepped in to take over the local business, Eric thought to himself. His mind drifted briefly to what Jackie Parton had told him, about the rumble of gang wars breaking out along the Tyne. Something danced into his mind at that moment, something Cheung had said, but he was unable to grasp it, fix its importance...

'So,' Pendragon announced, glancing at Dawes, 'it seems to me that we are now in a position, with the help of the Chinese embassy, to move forward with some expedition. And while we may offer thanks to Mr Ward, I feel sure we need involve him no longer in our deliberations.'

The deputy chief constable nodded, and looked at Eric. 'I'm afraid your lunch will be curtailed. But you appreciate we have ... operational matters to discuss. Your information will be followed up. I add all our thanks to Mr Pendragon's. DCI Spate ... perhaps you'd like to escort Mr Ward from the premises.'

Eric rose; Charlie Spate scraped his own chair back. 'Should I–'

Dawes nodded. 'We'll expect you back here. We still have a lot to discuss.'

Pendragon rose also, affably condescending. 'Before you go, Mr Ward, it hardly needs saying that we expect you to treat this meeting as confidential. And ... er ... our gratitude is heartfelt, in view of the difficult personal issues that have undoubtedly arisen for you in this matter. We appreciate your public-spiritedness. So ... you may expect to hear from one of my colleagues in the next few days. There are certain Treasury briefs that we might wish to take your opinion and action upon.'

As they walked out of the private room Spate was chuckling to himself. He said nothing as they entered the lift and made their way down to the entrance of the hotel, but there was an amused, cynical smile on his rugged features. As Eric stepped away from the lift and the automatic swing doors opened, Spate said, 'Well that was well done, Ward. You've gone up in my estimation.'

'What do you mean?'

Charlie Spate grinned at him, a lively cynicism dancing in his eyes. 'Well, not only do you help the police as any citizen should do, but you get a monkey off your back – me – and you make your time with the Home Office as well. Treasury briefs, hey? Everything's looking up, right? That'll pick up your business!'

'I'll see you around, Spate,' Eric said shortly and stepped forward through the doors.

As he did so he heard Spate laughing. 'And not only that, you cunning bugger!'

Eric stopped, looked back. 'What?'

'On top of all that, you get to shaft the guy who's been shagging your wife!'

Chapter Fourteen

It was just like the old days.

Then it had been a nightclub raid in the Isle of Dogs, or the storming of some sleazy hotel in north London, a charging up the concrete stairs of a decayed tower block, breaking up a bottle fight or conducting a running battle on slippery cobble-stones down by the river. Charlie Spate had enjoyed those early morning crashes, when they had kicked in a door, stormed through a house, dragged villains out of bed and hauled them off to the nick for questioning, along with an occasional thumping in the interests of justice. The early morning air had been crisp in his nostrils; the dark, damp streets had been quiet but heavy with subdued menace and hostility; the inevitable proximity of clatter and ensuing violence had given rise to a nervous tension that caused a knotting in the stomach, a shortness of breath until the signal came and they all piled out of the van and into the street. It was then that the tension changed, was dissipated and an adrenalin rush boiled them forward, yelling, intimidating, threatening so that the villains they sought had no time to catch their breath, respond, react, indulge in their own form of mindless, drug-coked violence.

And here he was again, ten years on from those heady, youthful excitements, sitting in the back of a truck with Chris Michaels and three other officers, waiting for the signal, feeling the build up of the old familiar tension in his veins. The occasional crackling radio contact was good: the team had now been spread out over several locations, and all were ready and waiting, watches synchronised so that no one jumped the gun and allowed the possibility that some birds might escape the nest. Linked up with the Cheshire and Manchester police everyone here was in place. *Operation Phantom*. One group were preparing to enter a country house at Alderley Edge where a celebratory dinner party had taken place hours earlier and where everyone should now be drunkenly snoring, and well abed with other men's wives; another was ready to storm a luxurious narrow boat on the River Douglas near Wigan, where two prime targets were entertaining their whores. A third operation was scheduled to surprise a few residents and alarm more than a few neighbours on the outskirts of Kingsmead in Northwich, all part of the UK operation. From the briefing, and the radio contacts, Charlie was aware that similar groups were in place, waiting for the co-ordinated signal in locations scattered through Germany and France and Spain. He glanced at his watch, looked up, caught Chris Michaels staring at him, a faint, edgy smile on his lips, the glint of anticipated battle in his eyes.

Charlie had reconsidered his view about the Australian. The previous day, after completion of the final operational briefing at Ponteland, Chris Michaels had surprised Charlie by suggesting they might have a drink together. With some hesitation mixed with a degree of suspicion, Charlie had agreed and they had walked into the village and found a quiet corner in a dark-beamed inn called The Royal Oak; Michaels had ordered the drinks, brought them across to the table and then seated himself opposite Charlie, staring directly and challengingly at him.

'You think I'm a bastard,' he asserted.

'I'm a copper. I work with whoever I got to,' Charlie replied coolly, not disputing the statement. 'Even Australians.'

The IMB man had nodded, and grinned lopsidedly. 'Fair enough, mate. I've never objected to blokes speaking their mind. But I thought maybe it was time we two got together to have a chat, so we could clear up any misapprehensions that might have come up these last weeks.'

'Is that what you call them? Misapprehensions?'

Charlie snorted in contempt.

Michaels glowered at him. 'Hey, I'm trying to build bridges here, mate. You see, you got to realise I've had a lot tied up in this operation. Four years of my life.'

'Not to mention the life of one of your own men,' Charlie replied, unmollified.

Chris Michaels was silent for a little while. 'Yeah, well ... you got to understand, that business with Sammy ... that was unexpected,' he conceded at last. 'We took him off the *Sierra Nova* when she was seized, put it about he'd been caught with drugs, but it was just a protective step. Hell, none of us thought the organisation would be stupid enough, so bloody reckless as to try to stick a knife in Sammy Edwards.'

'But they managed it.'

The Australian's eyes glittered with restrained malice. 'Yeah, and the bastards'll pay for it, too, believe me.' He scowled uncertainly at Charlie. 'I know you think I showed no reaction to that killing, that I was simply discounting his life, not allowing the incident to get to me, putting the broader picture first. And I suppose that you're right. But don't be misled into thinking that I didn't *care* about that killing. Sammy Edwards was one of my own men.'

Charlie shook his head doubtfully. 'Hell, you *all* seemed to think nothing about it. You didn't seem to want to do anything about the killing. You just covered it up, used your own people to damp everything down. Dammit, you and the DCC even slowed down our investigation, without even bothering to explain! And all that time I was supposed to be working with you, and I wasn't even told that Edwards was one of your own, working for the IMB!' He grunted in disgust, glared accusingly at the man sitting opposite him. 'And the same bloody situation with the Patsy Gullane killing. Nothing was to interfere with your sodding operation. Busting the syndicate was your main priority and everything else had to be sidelined. But I already gave you my views about that, you and the DCC.'

Michaels shuffled uncomfortably, and nodded. 'Okay, I hear you – and I heard you then. You had a point. But my hands – and the DCC was in the same position for that matter – our hands were more or less tied. Too much was riding on the situation: I was under pressure myself from above. You got to believe me I didn't like the way things had to be; you got to accept that the instructions were coming down from the IMB, from your own Home Office, from Pendragon, who was liaising with people in Germany and France and Spain, while the IMB itself co-ordinated the Asian side of things. And we had to take it carefully until we got the Chinese on board. This was always going to be an international operation. That meant we had to keep the lid on a lot of things until everything, and everyone was in place. You were one of the team, but on a need-to-know basis: the Home Office insisted that an operational officer was involved, but only up to a point.'

'That may be so, but–'

'We been four years setting all this up, and then right at the end it seems the whole thing was blown, with Sammy getting knifed. We couldn't risk any leaks, any possibility of the people we're after getting the wind up. It was bad enough that the people we were after had maybe located him, suspected that they were under surveillance. We had to let them think they'd succeeded in shutting Sammy's mouth, while we let the local force treat the issue as a drug-smuggling killing, until we got the last pieces in place.'

Reluctantly, Charlie shrugged, conceded the issue. He could see the logic of the argument. 'What was Edwards doing on board, anyway?'

'We planted him on board at Amsterdam, replacing another of our guys, just as a check. Nothing too obvious, just a way of keeping eyes and ears open, maintaining cellphone contact in case there was any change in the sailing schedules of the *Sierra Nova*. Advise us just who came on and off the freighter. We suspected she was a mother ship; we knew she was a phantom; and once we had her under lock and key at North Shields we were hoping to put the pressure on the owners, get them to break cover. This was just the UK end of the operation – and we had to get the doors open by getting the Chinese to co-operate.'

'Henry Cheung.' Charlie sipped his Foster's – the IMB man had given him no choice, merely assumed that Charlie drank the Australian brew – and recalled the smooth, unreadable features of the moon-faced embassy man. 'Just where do they fit into it all?'

'The Chinese? Hah,' Michaels muttered disgustedly. 'They've been a main source of problems for us all along. Ever since China took over Hong Kong, and for some years before that in fact, there's been a major problem with shipping in the South China Sea. Once ships were outside territorial waters they were anyone's game. There were Chinese patrol boats boarding freighters, cargo ships, threatening, stealing ... the authorities denied the stories, insisted that these were rogue elements beyond their control, pirates masquerading as officials, but all the while we knew they were turning a blind eye to what was going on, money was changing hands, kickbacks so that high up officials in the government would look the other way.'

'International protests?'

'Came to nothing. Beijing just denied it was anything to do with them.' Michaels stared at his lager gloomily. 'And the scams got worse, got better organised, and then the whole thing became just too serious, with the phantom ships becoming a major problem. You see, Charlie, in the beginning it used to be just looting the captain's safe, grabbing payrolls or port fees – though that alone could come to thousands of dollars – but in this last five years they upped the ante considerably. It was inevitable really: one third of the world's commercial shipping passes through the South China Sea like a conveyor belt of opportunity to the greedy, merciless sons of whores ashore. Two hundred incidents last year alone: and now it's a matter of entire ships and their cargoes, and crews getting massacred. The *Petro Ranger*, that was the watershed. Hell, three million dollars got hijacked there! That incident got everyone together, believe me, mate; the Malaysians, the Indonesians, the Thais, Singaporean and European shipping companies, they all realised something had to be sorted. At government level.'

'But you had to buy the co-operation of the Chinese?'

'Purchase,' Michaels agreed, 'and pressure. When we took the *Pulau Tengah* a few months back we netted a guy called Charlie Minh who was prepared to talk his head off. What we got from him – though it was little enough really – tied in with what we managed to obtain from a turncoat pirate captain, name of Cheung Kiat.' He grunted in disgust and took a long pull at his lager. 'The bloody shipping agent himself committed suicide rather than talk.'

'Drastic,' Charlie commented dryly.

'Scared of his Chinese bosses,' Michaels said in a disgruntled tone. 'Anyway, the Chinese government was finally somewhat embarrassed when the IMB, using the information gained, made a formal diplomatic complaint to Beijing that it was allowing its ports to be used by pirates, in contravention of international maritime law. And it was made clear that the other governments concerned had had enough – their shipping was being plundered. That was when senior Chinese officials agreed to join us when we held an IMB meeting in Singapore – that's the conference where we discussed a whole range of measures, such as arming the crews. But it was clear we had to have a concerted effort, agreed at government level and co-ordinated by the International Maritime Bureau. That was when your own government finally got involved. They took on the responsibility of putting forward a united European view and impressed on

Beijing that the other European states were tied in.'

'That was the stick. So what was the carrot?' Charlie asked curiously.

'A big trade agreement, certain political gifts and recognitions, and Beijing was finally persuaded that it was in their own best interests to help stamp on all these corrupt officials lining their own pockets. Here in the UK, in the Chinese embassy, Mr Henry Cheung was finally ordered by his Beijing masters to collaborate – and that's how he came to the meeting the other day, prepared to give us names and places here in the UK. But I tell you, it's been a long haul.'

'So it seems.'

Chris Michaels was silent for a short while, then he added, 'And that's how we had to go carefully. But now we can reel all the bastards in. Including the one who put the knife into Sammy Edwards. We'll find out whether they did for him because they discovered he was an undercover agent, or because they just wanted to put out a warning, show they weren't prepared to have their own operations messed about or threatened by individual smuggling operations on the part of crew members.'

'So you don't really know why he was killed?' Charlie asked.

'We'll bloody well find out, believe me,' Chris Michaels snarled.

'And you've not yet identified the killer.'

'No, but once we get these big bastards, we'll get them to crack. There are ways,' Michaels said grimly.

The house they were waiting to raid was set in its own thickly-treed, sprawling grounds, protected by a high wall. The soft-soled men in black bala-clavas had already scaled the wall, rendered the security systems inoperative, and were waiting, crouched in the undergrowth near the main house. The man responsible for the UK end of the international hijacking syndicate was inside, blissfully unaware of the hammer blow that was about to descend: from the dossier Charlie Spate had now seen it was clear that Philip Ong had enjoyed twenty years of uninterrupted criminal activity from his Manchester base: his triad had been involved in drugs, prostitution, booze, pro-tection, illegal immigration. But these were now sidelines only. Some four years ago he had been recruited into the new international activity, in-volvement in the phantom ship business; he was the UK link, one of a group of men who con-trolled the individual nerve centres, cells that all formed part of the wider network. Cells that were all going to be destroyed, this night, in Germany and France and Spain. And here, in Manchester.

'Time to go,' Michaels announced grimly, checking his watch.

The truck started up with a throaty roar, its engine screaming and wheels spinning as the driver slammed on the accelerator. The men in the back braced themselves against the cold walls and held on as the vehicle thundered forward, smashed into the ornamental gates with a screeching of tor-tured metal. Charlie and the others were bounced sideways as the vehicle lurched, shuddered over the remains of the destroyed gate then picked up speed and hurtled the eighty metres of gravelled drive down to the house. It swung, wheels sending up a spray of small stones, screeched to a halt directly in front of the main entrance, the doors at the back of the truck were thrown open and they all piled out. As they did so, the front entrance to the house was suddenly flooded with light, the door was kicked open and a man came out, roaring defiance, with a shotgun in his hands. He was able to blaze away, discharging both barrels almost aimlessly into the darkness beyond the lights before he went down with a scream, clutching his left thigh where a SWAT bullet had taken him and he lay on the steps, dropping the shotgun, yelling in shock and pain as the men in black clambered over and past him. Someone in front of Charlie was screaming, *'Go, go, go!'*

A window shattered, the splintering of the glass followed immediately by a stunning explosion and a gust of acrid smoke. All was confusion. Charlie followed Chris Michaels as he ran into the house and the SWAT team spread out in the hallway, darting through to the back, charging up the stairs in pre-arranged sequence, kicking in the doors to left and right. The acrid smell of cordite stained the air; from upstairs there came the sound of shouting and another muffled explosion from a stun grenade. Then at the far end of the hall one of the SWAT team yelled to them, waved to Chris Michaels. The Australian turned, and he gestured to Charlie. They hurried forward, entering the room at the end of the hallway as the man in black stepped aside, ran back towards the stairs, still echoing to the sounds of violence and

205

mayhem above.

The room was elegantly furnished, thickly carpeted, dimly lit. Calmly seated at a desk near the fireplace, its paper-littered surface lit by a spot lamp, sat a heavily-built, middle-aged man of Asiatic appearance. He was dressed in a somewhat dated fashion, wearing a wine-red, quilted smoking jacket, and he observed them calmly as he sat there with a book in one hand, a cigarette in the other. He seemed oblivious, unmoved by the crashing of glass above, the noise and the clamour and the smoke swirling throughout the house. He could not have expected this, and though his pulse must have been beating at an alarming rate, he was clearly intent on letting no one present see that he was concerned.

'Mr Chang Lee Ong?' Chris Michaels asked curtly, advancing.

'I am Philip Ong, yes.' The middle-aged man lowered his head slightly; the spotlight shining through his sparse dark hair, shining on the scalp. He put the book down slowly, and ground his cigarette into an ornate ashtray in movements of great and measured deliberation. His speech was slightly accented, but precise. 'I imagine your documentation for this ... outrage ... will all be in order?'

'You can bet your sweet life on it,' Chris Michaels replied savagely. 'Now you want to come with us quietly, or you want a piece of what that gorilla at the door got? Believe me, it'd suit me fine if–'

He had no time to finish. At the far end of the room a door suddenly crashed open in the panelled wall; from the narrow anteroom beyond a man came hurtling. Charlie got a quick impression of the muscular assailant: a big man, sweatered, dark-coloured jeans, slamming into Chris Michaels and knocking him sideways. Philip Ong cast aside his controlled calmness; he was rising to his feet quickly, his chair scraping back, stepping away from behind the desk as the big man turned, headed for Charlie. His clenched fist was swinging at Charlie's head, but Charlie sidestepped the blow, grabbing at the man's wrist, swinging his assailant off balance, slamming him into the wall. From the corner of his eye he saw Chris Michaels struggling groggily to his feet, Philip Ong slipping quickly through the door into the anteroom, half closing it behind him and Charlie guessed there would be some way out through the anteroom, some way to get free of the house, a route created maybe years ago, against such a contingency as this. But Michaels was up, plunging after the owner of the house. Unsteady or not, he was in no mood to let the man he wanted escape.

Charlie had no more time to see what was happening: Philip Ong's bodyguard was at him again, hands scrabbling, nails tearing into Charlie's throat, heavy charging bulk pushing him backwards. Charlie's legs struck the desk and he went over sideways, but he twisted as he fell, pulling the big man with him and they rolled frantically on the deep, expensive carpet. The man was strong, and aggressive, tearing at Charlie's throat, trying desperately to head butt him. But Charlie had been here before; he had mixed it since he was a kid; there had been battles in the London streets as a teenager, and as a young copper he had never been averse to using licensed violence to subdue villains as big as this. He drove his knee into the man's lower stomach and heard the grunt; with a satisfied roar he slammed his elbow into the man's jaw and heard teeth crack. He twisted, rolled again, and he was on top, straddled his assailant, used his forearm to smash into the man's nose and he felt the grip loosened, heard heels beginning to drum on the carpet as blood sprayed redly over Charlie's shirt.

Yeah, he exulted as he drove again with his forearm, it was just like the old days.

Chapter Fifteen

When Eric returned to the office late in the afternoon Susie met him with a quizzical look. 'So, you returned the cheque to Goldwaters and I thought all was lost and the bad old days were back, but now we've just had the Home Office on the phone.'

'Treasury briefs?' Eric guessed.

'The same.'

It had always been a ploy on Pendragon's part, of course: a discreet way of buying Eric's discretion, tying him into legal activity with the Home Office. But Susie did not need to know that. She stood there expectantly, eyebrows raised. 'It's just talent,' Eric explained airily. 'In the end, it will out.'

'As long as it pays my wages,' she replied drily, 'I'll be the last to complain.'

'Anything else?'

She frowned, tapping a suspicious pencil against the desk 'That detective sergeant, Elaine Start. Are you in trouble? Or have you got something going with her?'

'I'm shocked, Mrs Cartwright!' Eric protested, half smiling.

'Well, she was here the other day,' Susie explained defensively. 'And she wants to see you again today. Seemed to regard it as a matter of urgency: couldn't wait until tomorrow. So eventually I arranged that she should come around after five this afternoon.'

'No explanation as to what she wants to talk about?'

'None that she'd discuss with me,' Susie Cartwright replied primly.

Elaine Start finally arrived rather later than she had suggested, and Susie was preparing to go home when the detective sergeant entered the office. Susie Cartwright frowned suspiciously at Eric. 'You want me to stay a while, Mr Ward? There might be something you'll need.'

'I don't think so, Susie,' Eric said firmly, as he ushered the policewoman into his room. 'I'm sure we can manage – and I promise to lock up after myself.'

'Be sure you do,' she warned grimly and left, a little stiff-backed. Elaine Start grinned at him as she took a seat in front of his desk. 'Do I detect a certain huffiness there?'

She looked good sitting in his room: dark skirt

and jacket, white shirt, brooch at her throat. Eric smiled. 'Susie thinks as an almost divorced man I shouldn't be talking to attractive women in my office at the approach of dusk.'

'Even coppers?'

'Even coppers. Especially ones not in uniform.'

'Ah, so that's when we get dangerous,' Elaine mused. 'Anyway, thanks for the attractive compliment ... and thanks for agreeing to see me. I thought I needed to ... well, have a chat about things. And you're a friend of Sharon Owen.'

Eric held up a hand, slightly irritated. 'We're acquaintances only. Somehow, it's getting about...' He shook his head. 'Anyway... So it's not the *Sierra Nova* business you want to see me about?'

'No.' Elaine Start's tongue flickered against her lips; she looked around her, seeming edgy, nervous, a little uncertain. 'No, the *Sierra Nova* case, well, we had a debriefing of a sort early this afternoon. The DCC himself, no less. He was sort of triumphant. The whole thing's been cracked, he told us, everyone in the bag. He stood down the whole team, in fact, told us everything's in hand.'

'Including the killing of the crew member?'

'All in hand. Everyone in the net, he said.' She frowned, uncertainty still staining her tones. 'And then DCI Spate rang in too. He sounded high as a kite. Just like a kid. He was in on it, you know – the raid in Manchester last night. And he sounded like he enjoyed the excitement. Told me he took a bit of a thumping himself, but he sounded just like a bairn who'd won his first fist fight. The operation was a resounding success it seems. Here in England, and on the Continent as well. Whole bunch of people pulled in. Including a guy called Chang Lee Ong, head of the UK side of things. Yes, the DCC and Charlie Spate, they both sounded as though it was all sealed. Cracked this international syndicate they've been on about. Done deal. Finished.'

She sat there silently for a little while. Eric waited, somewhat puzzled. At last, he asked reluctantly, 'I gave certain information to DCI Spate, regarding ... parties who might have been involved in the phantom ship operations. Is that why you've come to see me?'

She looked at him steadily. 'I did hear some rumours that one of your wife's companies might have been tied in with the *Sierra Nova*. I'm sorry about that. They'll be pursuing that line of enquiry, I'm sure. I hope it goes okay. But no, that's not the reason why I wanted to talk to you. In that matter, I guess investigations will continue for some time. It could be a while before links are established, papers sorted out, decisions made.' She stroked her cheek abstractedly, thinking. 'No, it's not that. The DCC told us to stand down. It means I have to concentrate on what's already on my plate ... we had a death recently, a guy killed in a lorry collision. He was smuggling cigarettes.'

'I saw some headlines in the newspaper,' Eric commented. 'Negligent police chase. That sort of thing. But as far as I can make out the fuss has all died down.'

She nodded. 'Largely because there was no police negligence. And the guy who was killed – he was called Flinders – he ran smack into a Daihatsu truck that we think had maybe been a

211

deliberate ... anyway, never mind that. That's something I got to go on with. No, it's having the investigation into the killing of Edwards brought to a halt ... that's what bothers me.'

Eric hesitated. 'The deckhand killing... Why do you think I can help?'

She was silent, drumming her fingers on the arm of her chair. 'Life was always simpler in the movies.'

Surprised, Eric asked, 'How do you mean?'

'Ha, I've got this funny obsession, you know. Old Hollywood movies. You name it, I can tell you who played in it. Even the bit players. Old actors, too. Like Victor Jory. You always knew he was a villain because he had a thin, mean face, and narrow eyes. And Marc Lawrence as well, because he had a pockmarked cheek, scar on his face. The villains always looked shifty. Or wore a black hat. I tell you, in the Hopalong Cassidy movies black hats were a dead giveaway.'

Eric smiled. 'I'm sure you're right, but–'

'Trouble is, in real life, things aren't that obvious,' she interrupted. 'You can never be quite sure who are the good guys, and who are the villains.'

There was no laughter in her eyes or her tone, and the conversation was not a casual one. There was an underlying problem that was bothering her: she was talking around it, as though reluctant to voice what was troubling her. Eric leaned forward, suddenly interested. 'What's this all about, Elaine?'

'It's about people being dismissive, for God's sake, and not prepared to listen, just because I'm a woman, or because I just got promoted!' She stopped, annoyed at the petulance of her own outburst. 'No, it's not that either.' She looked him straight in the eyes. 'The man who got killed, the crew member from the *Sierra Nova*. Did you know he was one of the good guys?'

Eric frowned, puzzled. 'I'm not sure I follow you. Surely, he was being charged with drug smuggling.'

'That's right. But it was a cover. I learned from the briefing this afternoon that he actually worked for the International Maritime Bureau. The DCC was quite eulogistic about him. Deserves a medal, laying down his life for the cause, that sort of insincere crap. I heard better speeches from Laurence Harvey in *The Alamo*. And you could never say *he* oozed sincerity.'

Eric thought back to the meeting he had been invited to by Spate. In that private room in the Malmaison Hotel something that struck him as odd had been said at one point, by Chris Michaels. Eric concentrated, thinking back. And at last he remembered... *That's how we managed to put one of our own people on board the Sierra Nova.* Eric now realised Michaels must have been talking about the murdered crewman.

'I'm still not sure what you're getting at,' he said slowly.

She hesitated, then reached to the handbag she had placed at her feet. She opened it, extracted a videotape and laid it in front of her, on Eric's desk. She stared at it contemplatively. 'In the movies, you usually know who the bad guy is, and you expect certain behaviour from him. It's how the whole thing is structured. Okay, if it's a murder mystery, the identity is cloaked but there are always clues – and it's almost never the butler, you know what I mean?'

'So?'

'So, like I said you expect certain behaviour from villains. And that tends to condition your thinking ... you make the assumptions you're *supposed* to. The hero, he's going to be heroic and he's going to win the girl at the end. I think maybe that's what's been the problem with Sammy Edwards.'

'I still don't follow...' Eric began slowly, though he had a glimmer of what she was driving at.

'Well, we thought Edwards was a bad guy, so we expected certain behaviour from him. But ... this is a tape, taken from a camera used by one of the Japanese tourists present at the law courts when it all happened. We've viewed it time and again, got it doctored by the guys in the lab, but we still can't get a good look at the man who knifed Sammy Edwards. But never mind that, for the moment. The important thing to bear in mind, it was that all the time we kept studying that tape, we thought Sammy Edwards was one of the black-hatted brigade. We hadn't been told the truth ... so we thought he was a bad guy. But he wasn't. He was IMB. He was one of the good guys. One of us.' She looked around the room. 'And you know what that means?'

Uncertainly, Eric asked, 'Some of our basic assumptions might be incorrect?'

'That's just right. You got access to a VCR here?'

He nodded, rose to his feet. 'In the back room.'

They went through to the small room at the rear of the building. Eric switched on the light, cleared away some files on the table, slipped the videotape into the machine and pressed the power button. A few moments later the screen came to greenly glowing life.

'Just watch the sequence,' Elaine suggested, leaning forward to press the start button.

They sat side by side without speaking as the tape whirred through the sequence. Eric heard again the background shouting from Patsy Gullane, the screaming and the hubbub of confusion as Sammy Edwards went down and Sharon Owen went crashing into the wall of the witness room. He saw again the red stains on the white shirt of the security officer. When it was over, Eric sat silently, frowning. Elaine reached forward, ejected the tape and inserted another. 'There's this tape also. Different tourist. Different angle. And to my mind, it raises a different question.'

Once again they sat watching as the tape whirred on. When it finished, Elaine sat back expectantly. 'So what do you think?'

Eric shook his head. 'It's not really possible to see the killer's face in either sequence.'

'That's not what I'm after,' Elaine Start said impatiently. 'What do you make out ... what's going on there?'

Eric was puzzled. 'I'm not sure. It's inconclusive.'

'Then let me put a point of view,' the policewoman sighed. 'Each time we've looked at the tapes, we've reached a certain conclusion. Either Sammy Edwards was simply trying to do a runner after he left the courtroom, taking advantage of the distraction provided by the Gullane woman,

215

or else he actually saw the knife in the hand of his assailant and was trying to get away.'

Eric grimaced doubtfully. 'It's difficult to see...'

'But these conclusions were reached,' Elaine interrupted, 'when we still thought Edwards was one of the bad guys. In other words, we thought he had good reason to do a runner. But we know now that he was really working for the International Maritime Bureau.'

'So he would have had no reason to run,' Eric said flatly. 'Which suggests that the first theory is blown out of the water.'

'And the second?'

'That he'd seen the knife, and was trying to avoid it?' Eric paused, uncertainly. 'I'm not so sure... Let's take another look at the second tape.'

Elaine Start grunted her pleasure at the suggestion. 'I've been trying to get people to do just that for the past week, but they all have a mindset, DI Hamilton thinks he already has all the answers, DCI Spate is obsessed with this *Sierra Nova* thing, and I've been getting nowhere. So, here we go...'

They watched the sequence again. Something stirred in Eric's veins, a slight shuddering *frisson,* as the first glimmering of doubt entered his mind. He leaned forward suddenly, pressed the freeze button. 'This is where he turns his head.'

'And?'

Eric stared at the screen, ran the sequence forward for a few frames. 'Now he plunges to the left. But that's ... crazy.'

'Why?' Elaine Start asked urgently.

Eric considered the matter for a few moments, frowning. 'Well, if we make the assumption that

216

the man coming into the shot at the left is the killer, partly obscured by one of the escorts–'

'Who were also IMB men,' Elaine commented grimly.

'–and if we assume that Edwards is *not* trying to escape from his escorts, but *has* seen the knife and is trying to avoid being killed...'

'Yes?'

'Then if he's wanting to avoid the knife, he's actually going the wrong way.' Eric looked at Elaine, puzzlement in his eyes. 'If he's seen the knife coming, the natural thing to do would have been to step away to the right, to avoid the attack. Instead...'

'He lurches to the left, knocks into Sharon Owen, sends her crashing into the wall where she hits her head and slumps down, and then falls himself, with the knife between his ribs.' She was silent for a moment, staring abstractedly at the screen in front of her. 'We got the knife of course, and there's still all hell on down at the courts, with security still making enquiries as to how the killer could have smuggled in the knife. The general view is that it was probably concealed in his shoe. And no prints on the weapon, of course. However, never mind that ... what do you make of it all? Bearing in mind Sammy Edwards was really one of the good guys.'

Eric was staring at the screen. He wound the tape back for a few seconds, then replayed the sequence again. It was there. He should have seen it before; they should all have seen it. But as Elaine Start had suggested, they were all of a mindset, their views conditioned by the background of what they believed to be the truth.

'I think that while Charlie Spate and the rest of them have been off chasing phantoms,' Elaine Start commented quietly, 'we've been chasing our own kind of phantom on this tape. Looking at it, but seeing something else. Sammy Edwards wasn't trying to escape from custody, was he? And he wasn't trying to get away from the knife, either.'

'No,' Eric agreed. 'He wasn't. He'd seen the knife, but he didn't move away from it. Instead...'

'He crashed into Sharon Owen, shouldered her into the wall.' Elaine Start raised questioning eyebrows.

Something cold seemed to touch the back of Eric Ward's neck. 'He crashed into Sharon to knock her away from the danger. And he took the knife thrust himself.'

Elaine sighed, nodding. 'As we know now, he was one of the good guys.'

'That means the knife was never meant for Sammy Edwards,' Eric concluded, holding her wide-eyed stare. 'It was really meant for Sharon Owen.'

'Edwards saw it, tried to stop it ... protect her... And took the knife himself.' Elaine Start sat back in her chair, nodding in satisfaction. 'I needed someone else to confirm it. None of my colleagues can be bothered with the tapes ... they've all made their minds up. *Operation Phantom* has clouded their judgement. They're all convinced that the IMB man was killed by a hitman paid for by the syndicate, the people who were operating the scam with the *Sierra Nova,* protecting their interests. And the more this guy Chang Lee Ong denies knowing anything about the Edwards killing, the more they'll insist he's lying. Because to them it all makes sense. Whereas really...'

'But why would anyone want to kill Sharon Owen? And take such a risk, in the law courts for God's sake?'

Elaine Start shrugged. 'There's only one way to find out. We'd better talk to her as soon as possible. See if she can come up with any ideas. You know where she lives?'

Eric shook his head. 'No, but Victoria Chambers have a twenty-four hours operation. They'll know where we can find her.'

He went back into his office. Elaine Start sat down again as he picked up the phone, dialled for Sharon Owen's chambers. There was a short conversation with the duty receptionist. When it was over, Eric put down the phone and looked at Elaine Start. 'She's not in Newcastle at the moment. A hearing, in London. But they've given me her mobile number. And she'll be coming back to Newcastle this evening. Just hold on...' He picked up the phone, dialled again, waited. He shook his head. 'She's not got the mobile switched on. What do we do now?'

'I think,' Elaine Start suggested slowly, 'We'd better make damn sure we're there to meet her, when she gets off the London plane.'

Chapter Sixteen

Eric checked with Newcastle Airport and discovered that there would be a flight due in from London at eight o'clock that evening. It meant that he and Elaine would have plenty of time for a coffee and a quick meal before they drove out to the airport terminal at Ponteland. Elaine suggested they should use her car, which was parked at Manor Chare. She would then be able to drop Eric off back at his apartment in Gosforth later: his own car would be safe enough where he'd left it, in the Dean Street car park overnight. Eric locked up the office and they made their way around the corner to Sabatini's. 'Settle for some pasta?' she asked.

'That'll suit me. My treat.'

The restaurant was almost empty. He ordered a spaghetti carbonara; Elaine decided upon a pizza. They ordered coffee to follow. While they waited, Eric thought again about the tapes. He shook his head. 'I don't understand ... why should anyone want to kill her?'

Elaine Start looked at him, with a hint of cynicism in her eyes. 'Who knows at this stage in the game? But you lawyers ... you do deal with some funny people. From my point of view, it's just infuriating that we've been spending so much time concentrating on the IMB business, and we've let slide something that's been staring us in the face, just because of our obsession with phantoms...'

'Hmm... Anything more on this guy Billy Leven?'

Elaine shook her head. 'He's skipped. Unless he's one of the people they expect to pick up in *Operation Phantom*. I think DCI Spate will be expecting that, but it's unlikely isn't it? If Edwards was killed protecting Sharon Owen, the killer wasn't really involved in the phantom ship business.'

'But Patsy Gullane was creating a disturbance, a distraction, and Billy Leven was her protector...'

'And maybe protected her straight into Border Mires later.' There was a grim determination in Elaine's tones. 'We have to talk to Ms Owen tonight, before any more mistakes are being made.'

They finished their meal, dawdled over coffee and finally made their way up the hill past Trinity House to Manor Chare to get Elaine's car. On the hillside she nodded across to the Tyne Bridge: the traffic across the river seemed to be at a standstill. 'Looks like there's a problem,' she muttered. 'Maybe there's a hold up on the motorway – we'd better stay away from it, and cut through the town. We've still plenty of time to get to the airport for Sharon Owen's arrival.'

She manoeuvred the car out of Manor Chare, dropped down into Broad Chare and the Quayside and climbed the hill again at Dean Street. At the Swan House roundabout she groaned: the road onto the motorway was at a standstill and she was forced to turn into Pilgrim Street. It was a bad mistake: the traffic was solid there also. She switched on the car radio and soon picked up traffic news: there had been a collision north of New Bridge Street and traffic was stationary in three directions – west, east and north. It would take an hour to clear the chaos. Elaine swore. 'We'll have to cut back, go through the town.'

Twenty minutes later they had got no further than Gallowgate. The accident on the motorway had resulted in a snarling up of traffic throughout the city and they were now trapped in a long queue of irritated motorists, some of whom occasionally let off steam by blaring their horns. 'I was hoping we could have got out by way of Claremont Road,' Elaine fumed. 'Now it'll have to be past Leazes Park.'

'I don't think it's going to make that much difference,' Eric replied, checking his watch. 'But unless we get moving soon, that plane will be arriving... Do you think maybe we should go straight to her home?'

'The address you were given is in Gosforth, isn't it?' Elaine Start shook her head. 'That means crawling right across town again. And she might not be going straight home anyway. Forget it. Let's take a chance on the airport ... hah, looks like we're moving at last!'

They edged forward. Elaine showed herself to be an expert driver: she took advantage of every opportunity, scraping through narrow gaps, swinging past hesitant motorists, until at last the A189 was clearing somewhat and they were able to pick up speed. 'It'll be tight,' Eric suggested.

'Maybe the plane won't be on time.'

With the city behind them they pressed on swiftly, swung into the road to the airport terminal. Elaine pulled in at the pick up point directly in front of the building. Eric got out, glancing at his watch. They were late. He hurried through the doors and checked the Arrivals board. The eight o'clock London flight had landed early, some twenty minutes ago. He had a word with the girl at the Information desk. It was her guess that the passengers would already have disembarked and left the terminal building. Eric walked swiftly back to the car. 'We've missed her.'

'Dammit!' Elaine thumped her hand on the steering wheel in frustration. 'That means we'll have to get to her place in Gosforth. Back into the traffic, my friend.'

'Take the back road,' Eric suggested, 'through Blagdon.'

Elaine nodded. She was familiar with the route. A few minutes later they were heading past Make Me Rich and out towards the Gosforth Road.

The delay had been unavoidable but Eric felt uneasy. Their viewing of the tapes had now convinced him that the attack at the Crown Courts had been directed at Sharon Owen and that meant she could still be in danger. He glanced at Elaine, intent behind the wheel. 'Since that attempt on her life failed that day, I wonder why no further attempt's been made against her.'

'I've been thinking about that myself,' Elaine replied soberly. 'The killer failed at the law courts, but Sharon was admitted to hospital with concussion, when Edwards slammed her sideways into the wall. She'd have been safe at the hospital. And when she was released, the heat was on, we were looking for Patsy Gullane, enquiries were being made–'

'Even if they were pretty low key.'

'Enough to decide that Patsy Gullane was a liability and had to be removed first... Anyway, now Spate and the rest of the team think it's all been wound up, and Sharon Owen is back in circulation–'

'She's been in London a couple of days.'

'But she's back in Newcastle now,' Elaine asserted grimly.

They were driving into Gosforth High Street. Elaine slowed, peering around her. She asked Eric for the address again, then swore as she realised she'd passed the appropriate turning. She swung into a side street, reversed, pulled back into the High Street. 'We'll need to take a left somewhere down here,' she muttered.

A few moments later she grunted with satisfaction and turned right. The houses were Victorian, double-fronted, in the upper bracket price range. As they drove slowly along, seeking the correct house number, ahead of them Eric caught sight of a taxi, double parked, just beginning to pull away with its indicators winking. 'Maybe that's the cab she took from the airport. That'll be her house there.'

'Where the hell can I stop?' Elaine asked, irritated. 'The whole damn street is full of parked cars.'

She slowed to a crawl, seeking an available space. Eric looked out of the side window, saw the lights come on in the double-fronted house, caught a glimpse of a woman entering the hallway. It looked like Sharon Owen. 'There she is.

Okay, Elaine, just drop me here,' he suggested. 'You go on, find a place to park and I'll–'

He stopped abruptly. Sharon Owen was framed in the doorway, the light behind her, but as she turned there was someone else there on the steps, tall, heavily built, hand outstretched. He was pushing her into the hallway. 'Bloody hell!' Elaine Start snarled, and slammed on the brakes.

Eric leapt out of the car. As he did so he heard the roar of a car engine, and a vehicle pulled out from the kerbside on the other side of the road. He looked back, caught a glimpse of a pale face framed in the window before the car thundered down the road, away from them. Elaine shouted something, as she fumbled in the glove compartment in front of the passenger seat but Eric hardly heard her. He was up and running, heading down the pathway towards the house. The door was just closing as he reached it: he thrust out his hand, pushed it open, stumbled inside.

The hallway was long and narrow, stairs ascending to the right, a door open at the far end, leading into the kitchen. As he burst in, it was like a frozen tableau before him. Sharon Owen was on her knees, slumping sideways, dazed, crying out, whimpering in pain. The man who stood over her, gripping her by the wrist, seemed shocked into stillness. Then he turned his head, glared at Eric, and released her wrist, half turned. Eric caught a glimpse of the man's reddish hair in the hall light before he charged.

Even as he slammed into the hard body of Sharon's assailant Eric knew he was in trouble. His antagonist stumbled, rocked backwards, colliding with the door, but did not go down. Instead, Eric found himself swung about, neck encircled by a powerful arm, hard muscle clamping his throat, and then the breath was driven out of his body as a fist hit him fiercely in the solar plexus. He gasped for air, winded by the blow, and his senses swam. He tried desperately to pull away from the throttling arm, scrabbled at the man's body but it was useless; the man was younger, stronger and as another blow came at Eric, striking him on the side of his head he staggered backwards, dazed, the encircling arm still making him fight for air. He could hear someone shouting, screaming, but the words were whirling about him, unrecognisable as he felt the pain starting behind his eyes, the old familiar pain, and his vision blurred, and then suddenly he was falling backwards, twisting, but the strangling arm was no longer there, he was released, dropping to his knees.

He stayed where he was for what seemed an age, fighting for breath, stars flashing in the blackness behind his eyes, aware that someone was beside him but unable to focus as a fierce pain raged in his head and eyes, and he coughed and hawked, his eyes streaming with tears. The words became clearer, intelligible. 'Eric, you all right? Sorry about that...'

Someone was dragging at him, pulling him away. Through a mist of tears and pain he squinted up and saw Elaine Start. 'It's okay Eric, we got the bastard!' she announced triumphantly.

From the entrance to the kitchen Eric could hear the sound of violent coughing and retching. Through blurred eyes he could make out his assailant, big, red-haired, also on his knees, hands braced on the floor, helplessly coughing with his head down. Sharon Owen was getting up, edging towards them past her helpless attacker, as they stood there in the passageway.

'Are you all right, Sharon?' he heard Elaine Start ask.

White-faced, shaking, she nodded assent.

Elaine Start had her arm around Eric's waist. She waved something at him, a small canister. 'CS gas,' she explained. 'I keep it in the glove compartment of my car. Not supposed to, of course, but what's a girl to do if she's likely to meet scumbags like this one.'

Eric looked at the big, red-haired man kneeling helplessly in the kitchen of Sharon Owen's home. 'Is that ... is that Billy Leven?'

'The very same, is my guess,' Elaine replied grimly. 'I'll be ringing now, to call for backup. He's got some explaining to do.'

Eric wiped his eyes with the back of his hand. He'd been lucky that the gas which had caused Leven to release him had only affected him lightly. 'There was a car in the street,' he said. 'It shot off when we arrived, after Leven forced his way into the house. Did you see who it was?'

She shook her head. 'No. Did you?'

He nodded. Viciously, he said, '*He's* going to have some explaining to do, as well. Like why he was tied in with Leven, why he brought Leven to this house, and just why they both wanted Sharon out of the way.'

'So who was it?' Elaine asked, puzzled.

'Someone both Sharon and I know. Someone

who had actually briefed her on behalf of a man called Joe Tilt.'

'Briefed her?' Elaine sounded puzzled. 'You mean the man who drove Leven here is a lawyer?'

Eric nodded coldly. 'Exactly that. A shyster called Teddy Archer.'

Chapter Seventeen

Before retirement, the Chief Constable was expecting the award of an honour. Feelers had already been put out and he felt he deserved the accolade: he had had a fine career, there were no major blots on his escutcheon, and he held the respect of those who counted in the north-east and in Whitehall, too. And in his view he ran a tight organisation. But the smoothness of the operation relied upon the detailed work being done by his minions, under his general direction, and he resented being dragged into consideration of minutiae. He had passed on the instructions from the Home Office to his deputy, and he had expected everything to be undertaken with efficiency and despatch. So he was not pleased, now that the reports suggested all had not gone as well as he would have expected. His deputy had not been sufficiently well on top of the task given him. And if he was to retain the chance of an honour, he needed to keep things running well. No hitches.

The Chief Constable was the only one seated in the room. DS Elaine Start and DCI Charlie

Spate stood in front of the Chief's desk; Deputy Chief Constable Dawes had been instructed to stand also, just to the right of his boss, facing the two officers, and he was clearly uncomfortable at the situation. As he had every bloody right to be, the Chief Constable thought sourly. Keep the bugger standing; show him his place.

'So where is DI Hamilton?' the Chief Constable rasped.

Charlie Spate offered the explanation. 'He's in London, sir. A conference with the IMB people. Sorting out the whole international business. I thought it best to let him—'

'IMB. Never mind that. Is this man Archer talking?' the Chief Constable interrupted in freezing tones.

'For a lawyer,' Charlie Spate suggested, 'he's being remarkably helpful. But then, he seems to think that if he can lay it all off on other people, maybe the fact that he is a lawyer will help him.'

'And will it?'

Before Charlie Spate could reply, Elaine Start shook her head, and intervened. 'He's in the whole business right up to his neck. Indeed, my guess is that it all came about because of his own panicky reaction to threats from Joe Tilt.'

'You'd better explain,' the Chief Constable suggested with a weary air, as Dawes shuffled uneasily at his side, uncertain whether to interject, take over explanations and make excuses, or leave it to the detective sergeant to dig the hole.

Elaine Start shot a quick glance at Charlie Spate, hesitating; he scowled at her, but said nothing. She'd jumped in with both feet. This was her show.

'It all revolves around the fact that Teddy Archer had been retained for some time by Joe Tilt, who as we know now, not only has his fingers in various criminal activities along the river, but has been actively seeking to expand his business.'

'At the expense of other operations, I presume,' the Chief Constable offered.

'Yes, sir, that's it exactly. One of the ... expansions ... related to an attempt to take over food distribution deals to the restaurants in the north-east. The supplies included alcohol and cigarettes as well as food, and much of it was being smuggled in from Europe. It was a lucrative business, and Joe Tilt was muscling in. There had been hints of strong arm tactics made in the newspapers – Tilt faced them down, or threatened them to keep their mouths shut. Successfully. That bit of business was handled by Eric Ward. But one of Tilt's targets, his rivals Northern Foods Limited, decided to take Tilt on in court. Tilt retained Teddy Archer. Archer prepared the defence papers. He briefed a young barrister–'

'Sharon Owen?' the Chief Constable asked.

'That's right, sir. But Archer made a bad mistake. When he prepared the file for her, he inadvertently left in the file some notes he had made during an earlier meeting with Joe Tilt. The notes amounted to a transcript of a taped discussion he'd had with Tilt.'

'Taped discussion?' the Chief Constable frowned.

She nodded. 'Tilt discussed the whole Northern Foods business with Archer. But Tilt didn't know the discussion in Archer's office was being taped.'

'Why did Archer tape it anyway?'

'Archer was always looking for an edge, even in his relationship with Tilt. He was also wanting to protect his back. Dealing with people like Tilt, he wanted to be sure he would have his own protective materials, if things ever turned ugly.'

'And this taped discussion...?'

Elaine Start took a deep breath. 'DCI Spate had asked me to head up a liaison group with Customs and Excise. The cigarette run, you know, sir. The lorry driver – Flinders – who was killed in the collision with the Daihatsu. Well, as I've already intimated, it seems that the cigarette smuggling was something Joe Tilt was wanting to horn in on. There's been a bit of a gang war rumbling on over it. And it was Tilt who arranged for the Daihatsu to ram the cigarette lorry. It was all part of the battle with Northern Foods – they were the ones organising the runs. And the Daihatsu business, it was the subject of a discussion between Archer and Tilt.'

'Which Archer taped?'

'And a transcript of which he inadvertently left in the briefing documents he gave to Sharon Owen.'

'Why didn't he just get the transcript back from her?'

Charlie Spate had had enough of leaving the limelight to his detective sergeant. 'We've talked to her,' he asserted. 'He did try, but she'd removed the papers as irrelevant to the case she was working up. And he was afraid she would have read them, and Tilt was suspicious, and if the information had got out Archer knew what

231

Tilt would do. So he got hold of Billy Leven–'

'You mean it was this lawyer Archer who set Leven at Sharon Owen?' the Chief Constable asked in disbelief.

'He was panicked,' Elaine Start intervened.

'He over-reacted,' Charlie Spate added, glowering at her. 'It was stupid, but he ... yes, panicked. Archer's story is that he simply asked Leven to sort it out, stressed the urgency of stopping her talking about the transcript, but didn't mean for the big thug to be so stupid as to try knifing her in the law courts building. But Billy Leven was never one of the brightest stars intellectually: keeping someone quiet in his book meant shutting them up permanently. So, he got his girlfriend Patsy Gullane to start a rumpus outside the crown courtroom, and in the chaos that followed he went for the barrister. But he got Sammy Edwards instead.'

'The man from the International Maritime Bureau,' the Chief Constable intoned, turning his cold eyes on his deputy. Dawes shuffled in discomfort, opened his mouth, but thought further and decided discretion was called for. He remained silent.

'And then, later,' Spate continued after a short pause, 'when Archer got mad at him for bungling the job, and exposing them both, with Joe Tilt getting even more suspicious, Leven thought it best tried to cover his own back, settle matters by disposing of Patsy Gullane, afraid she'd blow the whistle if she got caught... He'd heard she'd been identified, the crack on Tyneside was that we were looking for her...'

'So he killed her, and dumped her in Border Mires,' Elaine added.

'But Teddy Archer was still left with the problem of Sharon Owen. He called in at her chambers, but she had the files with her in hospital and wouldn't hand them over until she'd finished working up the case against Northern Foods. When Archer finally collected them from Victoria Chambers, he realised the transcript wasn't among the papers. That transcript was his insurance against trouble from Tilt, and if the Owen woman had read them, understood the implications, the link could be made between Joe Tilt, Teddy Archer and the gang war, the killing of the man driving the Northern Foods cigarette run... He made up his mind that maybe Leven had been right, that the safest way out of the problem was to make sure she didn't ever talk about it. So he sent in Billy Leven a second time.'

'Actually, he *took* Leven to the Owen house in Gosforth,' Elaine Start corrected him insistently, 'rather than sent him in.'

'Which is where you came in,' the Chief Constable commented, his lids hooding as he observed the detective sergeant carefully. 'Just as well there was *someone* around who could see the wood for the trees. The rest of the troop were out chasing phantoms, ignoring a killing that was there under their noses.'

'That's not quite fair, sir,' Dawes began to protest. 'Your instructions, the Home Office directive...' His words died away when the Chief Constable's cold eyes turned to him.

'You were working under that directive from

the Home Office, I understand that,' the Chief Constable conceded reluctantly. 'But I would still expect the team to exercise their common sense. Following the directive shouldn't have been at the expense of keeping your eyes open, looking at the evidence before you, not assuming everything was tied in to the phantom ship business. Now, it turns out, you were all off on a wild goose chase, there was no real connection–'

Charlie Spate stiffened. He was not in the business of protecting DCC Dawes, but a wild goose chase, it hadn't been. 'That's not quite right, sir.'

The Chief Constable's chin came up threateningly. 'What's that, Spate?'

'Connection. There was a connection.'

'Tell me,' the Chief Constable ordered unbelievingly.

'Tilt was trying to muscle in on a food distribution racket, and a smuggling operation involving booze, cigarettes, and, we believe, illegal immigrants. That was what Northern Foods were doing. But the company itself...'

'Yes?' the Chief Constable demanded in a tone stained with belligerence.

'It was one of Chang Lee Ong's companies. A front. Part of the criminal activity he'd been indulging in for years, from his Manchester base. Nothing to do directly with the phantom ship operation, of course, or the *Sierra Nova*. But there was a connection, after all ... and once we'd got our hands on the main players, the major villains, we'd have got around to it eventually.'

'Only by then that lawyer woman would have been long disposed of,' the Chief Constable argued, snorting his disagreement. His pale eyes shifted to look again at Elaine Start. 'We still owe a great deal to this young woman. You look after her, DCI Spate. She'll be going places. But for now...' He waved a hand in dismissal. 'I'll expect a written report from you both. Now, if you'll leave us ... I have a few things to discuss with Mr Dawes...'

As they walked down the corridor, with the sound of raised voices in the office behind them, Spate muttered, 'Sounds like Dawes is getting the bollocking he deserves, as well.' He shot a sly glance at the detective sergeant. 'But you, smelling of roses, hey? Leaving the poor peasants, DI Hamilton and DCI Spate trudging through the manure back at the farm. And I got to look after you!'

'Not in the way you'd like, I'm sure,' she suggested.

He stopped at the door to his office. 'You reckon there's enough to make charges stick against Archer, as well as Leven?'

She shrugged. 'Archer might cop a plea, and I have a feeling we'll have a smart lawyer arguing the case for Joe Tilt. We got the tape, and he won't wriggle out of the Flinders case, but his lawyer will be denying Joe Tilt's involved in any way in the attack upon Sharon Owen, and the killing of Edwards or Patsy Gullane. That's down to Archer and Leven. And *their* smart lawyer.'

'But not a lawyer like Eric Ward,' Charlie Spate suggested.

Elaine smiled. 'No. Certainly not Eric Ward.'

Two weeks later, in The Treacle Moon restaurant

at the Side in Newcastle, enjoying a lunch at Eric Ward's expense and seated beside Sharon Owen, the thought returned to Elaine Start. 'Teddy Archer is singing his heart out, giving us access to all his files freely, trying to do his best to get Tilt banged up inside. Queen's Evidence is his best bet, otherwise he suspects he could be ending up with a knife in his stomach like Sammy Edwards, if Tilt actually walks free.'

Sharon Owen shuddered. 'I still get nightmares about that evening. And you know, that transcript, I'd seen it, read it, but it didn't really make sense to me. I put it to one side, left it at home, didn't put it back in the file and really, just forgot about it. So when Leven came charging into the house, after the transcript and me ... I just didn't know what was going on.'

'No matter,' Elaine Start said. 'We have the transcript now, and if we can get it introduced into evidence, we'll see Archer, Leven and Tilt in the dock. Still, I reckon that's enough about all that. It's nice of you to invite me to lunch, as a thank you, Eric. When you could have been here just with Sharon.'

Eric Ward laughed uneasily, glanced at the young barrister. Everyone seemed to be suggesting that he and Sharon were becoming something of an item. He hesitated, met Elaine Start's eye. 'The invitation to lunch, it's not just a thank you, really. I'd hoped to get some information out of you.'

'About what?'

'Lincoln Shipping,' Eric replied carefully. 'Jason Sullivan ... and my ex-wife.'

'Divorce through, then?' Elaine asked.

Eric nodded. 'But I've been wondering...'

Elaine Start understood. 'Well, I can tell you that the IMB investigation is proceeding well. They've got most of the main players under lock and key, including Chang Lee Ong, head of the UK branch of the syndicate, and, of course, organiser of the Northern Foods scams. Charlie Start tells me they're having more difficulty with the *Sierra Nova* Singapore contracts. The guy who retained you–'

'Paul Sutherland,' Eric supplied.

'He's been interviewed at length, of course, and I'm afraid that's caused a bit of rustling in the dovecotes. I hear Sutherland's now been given the push by Goldwaters, for getting them involved with the *Sierra Nova* business in the first place, and then not keeping them up to speed with the problems.'

'So there goes his shares bonus,' Eric muttered, 'and his aspirations.'

'As for Jason Sullivan, he's still being questioned over Lincoln Shipping. Charlie tells me he's not sure whether Chris Michaels is really going to have enough on Sullivan to press charges, but I hear on the grapevine that Lincoln Shipping is being deregistered, closed down by the Singapore government.'

'And Morcomb Enterprises?'

Elaine shrugged. 'Will walk away clean, that's my guess. Sullivan has stepped down from the board. And there's nothing to suggest that your ... ex-wife was in any way culpable, or even knew what was going on. We're not even sure we can pin anything on Sullivan himself, for that matter. But he's been in trouble with his Benchers before ... and I think this will sink him, even if we don't find enough to bring charges against him. Mud sticks...'

They finished their lunch, talking no more of the *Sierra Nova,* or the events that had surrounded it. Elaine Start entertained them with anecdotes about her DCI, and suggested that he was trying to model himself on Humphrey Bogart. 'But you know, he hasn't got the charisma or the lisp ... and if he whistled–!'

'You wouldn't do a Lauren Bacall?' Eric asked with a grin.

She rose to her feet. 'I've never been the sultry, light me a cigarette type,' she announced, smiling. 'But that's my mobile going, and I think it gives me my cue, to exit left.'

After she had gone, Eric called for the bill. He glanced at Sharon Owen. 'Detective Sergeant Elaine Start ... that's a woman who can look after herself.'

'Unlike some you could mention?'

He looked at Sharon. For a moment he suspected the darkness behind the question in view of her recent experiences, but there was the hint of laughter in her eyes. And something else too, a mockery, a hint. She was a very beautiful young woman, he concluded. 'Oh, I think you have the kind of strength that Elaine has.'

'That doesn't mean I don't need looking after,' she teased him.

He smiled. 'No, I suppose not. Perhaps, indeed, you do.' But whether he was the right person to do that was something he was not prepared to contemplate. At least, not at this point in time.

The publishers hope that this book has given you enjoyable reading. Large Print Books are especially designed to be as easy to see and hold as possible. If you wish a complete list of our books please ask at your local library or write directly to:

Magna Large Print Books
Magna House, Long Preston,
Skipton, North Yorkshire.
BD23 4ND

This Large Print Book for the partially sighted, who cannot read normal print, is published under the auspices of

THE ULVERSCROFT FOUNDATION

THE ULVERSCROFT FOUNDATION

... we hope that you have enjoyed this Large Print Book. Please think for a moment about those people who have worse eyesight problems than you ... and are unable to even read or enjoy Large Print, without great difficulty.

You can help them by sending a donation, large or small to:

**The Ulverscroft Foundation,
1, The Green, Bradgate Road,
Anstey, Leicestershire, LE7 7FU,
England.**
or request a copy of our brochure for more details.

The Foundation will use all your help to assist those people who are handicapped by various sight problems and need special attention.

Thank you very much for your help.